Lorna Doone

D0733994

LORNA DOONE

R. D. Blackmore

Edited and abridged by Doris Dickens

Illustrations by Michaela Stewart

First published in 1879

This illustrated edition first published
in Armada in 1988
This edition published 1993 by
Diamond Books
77-85 Fulham Palace Road
Hammersmith, London, W6 8JB

© text in this edited and abridged edition
Doris Dickens 1988

© illustrations Michaela Stewart 1988

All rights reserved

Printed and bound in Great Britain

Conditions of Sale
This book is sold subject to the condition
that it shall not, by way of trade or otherwise,
be lent, re-sold, hired out or otherwise circulated
without the publisher's prior consent in any form of
binding or cover other than that in which it is
published and without a similar condition
including this condition being imposed
on the subsequent purchaser.

Introduction

Having seen a performance of a classic work of literature on television, children are often disappointed and frustrated when they find they are unable to read and understand the original. With this in mind, Doris Dickens, great-granddaughter of Charles Dickens and a former teacher, has edited and abridged many well-known books including *Oliver Twist*, *The Old Curiosity Shop*, *The Children of the New Forest*, *Little Men*, *Dracula* and now *Lorna Doone*.

This is not *Lorna Doone* retold but "a simple tale told simply", as R. D. Blackmore intended.

Chapter I

If anybody cares to read a simple tale told simply, I John Ridd, of the parish of Oare, in the county of Somerset, yeoman and churchwarden, have seen and had a share in some doings of this neighbourhood which, God helping me, I will now relate.

My father, John Ridd the elder, being a great admirer of learning and well able to write his name, sent me his only son to be schooled at Tiverton, in the county of Devon. In that town there is a worthy grammar school, the largest in the west of England, founded in the year 1604 by Master Peter Blundell of Tiverton, clothier.

I was a strong boy and won many fights and was doing well at my lessons in the first form of the upper school when, at the age of twelve, I was called away from learning and this was how it happened:

Another boy and I were having a fight after school when, not from the way of Taunton, but from the side of

Lowman bridge, came our red-faced farm-hand John Fry, riding a horse and leading my pony Peggy. He had come to fetch me.

"Oh, John, John," I cried, "what's the use of your coming now, and bringing Peggy over the moors, too, and it is so cruel cold for her? The holidays don't begin till Wednesday, John. To think of your not knowing that!"

John Fry leaned forward in the saddle, and turned his eyes away from me, and then there was a noise in his throat, like a snail crawling on a window-pane.

"Oh, us knows that well enough, Master John. Your mother have kept all the apples up, and old Betty have turned the black puddings and none dare set trap for a blackbird. All for thee, lad, every bit of it now for thee!"

He checked himself suddenly and frightened me. I knew John Fry's way so well.

"And father, oh how is father?" I pushed away some boys who had gathered round as I said it. "John, is father up in town? He always used to come for me, and leave nobody else to do it."

"He couldn't leave home by reason of the Christmas bacon coming on and the cider to make."

He looked between the horse's ears as he said it, and, being up to John Fry's ways, I knew that it was a lie. And my heart fell, like a lump of lead, and I leaned back against the gate. A cloud hung over me and I feared to be told anything. I did not even care to stroke the nose of my pony Peggy although she was nuzzling at me.

"Take me to thy Master, lad, and get leave to go," said John. One boy held his horse Smiler and another held Peggy, while John saw the Master and I waited outside the room. Leave was given at once and we went back to the boys and mounted. My heart was heavy and a dullness hung over me as I left my school and friends for ever.

Chapter II

From Tiverton town to the town of Oare is a very long and painful road and in the days of my schooling it was pretty well unmade and it was a sad and sorry business to find where lay the highway. We lodged one night at the White Horse Inn in Tiverton to rest the horses and set off at cockcrow the next morning.

Still John Fry would not tell me the reason of his coming and only told lies about father which did not ease my mind at all. I just hoped for the best and thought perhaps father had sent for me because he had a good harvest, and the rats were bad in the corn-chamber.

It was high noon before we got to Dulverton that day, near to which town the River Exe and its big brother Barle have union. My mother had an uncle living there, but we were not to visit his house this time, at which I was somewhat astonished, since we would need to stop at least two hours to feed and water the horses and rest them. We dined well at Dulverton on mutton pasty and, from time to time, John Fry glanced at me as if he were sorry about something, but he said little. I went into the town to buy some sweetstuff for my sister Annie and we left Dulverton, turning into a sideway soon afterwards. The road got worse and worse, until there was none at all as if it were ashamed to show itself, but we pushed on as best we might, with doubt of reaching home any time, except by special grace of God.

The fog came down upon the moors as thick as ever I saw it and there was no sound of any sort, nor a breath of wind to guide us. The little stubby trees that stand here and there, like bushes with a wooden leg to them, were drizzled with a mass of wet, and hung their tops and soon it was too dark to see them or anything else, I may say, except the creases in the dusk, where little bits of light crept up the valleys.

After a while even that was gone, and no other comfort left to us, except to see our horses' heads jogging to their footsteps, and the dark ground pass below us, lighter where the wet was, and then the splash, foot after foot, more clever than we can do it, and the orderly jerk of the tail and the smell of what a horse is.

John Fry was bowing with sleep upon his saddle, and now I could no longer see the frizzle of wet upon his red beard, but I could just make out the jog of his hat and his shoulder bowed out in the mist as I cried out, "Hold up, John!" when Smiler stumbled into a hole.

"Mercy of God! Where are we now?" said John Fry, waking suddenly. "We ought to have passed the old ash, John. Seen it on the road, have you?"

"No indeed, John, no old ash. Nor nothing else to my knowing, nor heard nothing save you snoring."

"What a fool thee must be then, John, and me myself no

10

better. Harken, lad, harken!"

We drew our horses up and listened, through the thickness of the air, and with our hands laid to our ears. At first there was nothing to hear, except the panting of the horses, and the trickle of the drips from our hats and clothing, and the soft sounds of the lonely night, that make us feel and try not to think. Then there came a low and mournful noise and I touched John Fry to know that there was something ahead of us.

"Don't be a fool, John, 'tis but the man in chains swinging ahead there."

"Have they hanged one of the Doones then, John?"

"Hush lad, no chance of that. Hang a Doone! The King himself would hang if they dared."

"Then who is in the chains, John?"

"It be nobody," said John, "as to make a fuss about. Belongs to the other side of the moor and came stealing sheep on our side. Red Jem Hannaford's his name. Thank God for him to be hanged, lad, and God rest his soul for showing us the way with his creaking."

So the sound of the quiet swinging led us on as it came and went on the wind even as far as the foot of the gibbet where the four crossways are.

John Fry shook his bridle-arm, and touched up Smiler merrily as he jogged into the homeward track from the guiding of the body. But I was sorry for Red Jem, and wanted to know more about him, and whether he might not have avoided this miserable end, and what his wife and children thought of it, if indeed he had any. But John would talk no more about it, and perhaps he was moved with a lonesome feeling as the creaking sound came after us.

"Hold thy tongue, lad," he said sharply, "we be near the Doone track now, two miles from Dunkery Beacon hill,

11

the highest place of Exmoor. If they be out tonight, we must lie low, boy."

I knew at once what he meant – those bloody Doones of Bagworthy, the terror of all Devon and Somerset, outlaws, traitors, murderers. My legs began to tremble to and fro upon Peggy's sides, as I heard the dead robber in chains behind us, and thought of the live ones still in front.

We had come to a long trough among the hills and rode very carefully down our side and through the soft grass at the bottom, while all the time we listened. Then gladly we started to climb the other side and were near the top when I heard something and caught John's arm, and he bent his hand to the shape of his ear. It was the sound of horses' feet, knocking up through splashy ground as if the bottom sucked them. Then a grunting of weary men, and the lifting noise of stirrups, and sometimes the clank of iron, the creak of leather and the blowing of hairy nostrils.

"God's sake, John, slip off and let Peggy go where she will."

As John Fry whispered, so I did, for he was off Smiler by this time, but the horses were too fagged to go far and began to nose about and crop, sniffing more than they need have done. I crept to John's side very softly, with the bridle on my arm.

"Let go the bridle, let go, lad. Please God they take them for forest ponies or they'll send a bullet through us."

I saw what he meant and let go the bridle, for now the mist was rolling off, and we were against the skyline to the dark cavalcade below us. John lay on the ground in some heather, where a little gullet was, and I crept to him, afraid of the noise I made in dragging my legs along and the creak of my cord breeches. John bleated like a sheep to cover it – a sheep very cold and trembling.

Then, just as the foremost horseman passed, scarce

12

twenty yards below us, a puff of wind came up the glen, and the fog rolled off before it. And suddenly a strong red light, cast downwards by the weight of the clouds, spread like fingers over the moorland, opened the alleys of darkness and flashed on the steel of the riders.

"Dunkery Beacon," whispered John. "Why, what be about, lad?"

For I could keep still no longer, but wriggled away from his arm, and along the little gullet, still going flat on my chest and thighs, until I was under a grey patch of stone, with a fringe of dry fern round it. There I lay, scarce twenty feet above the heads of the riders, and I feared to draw my breath though I was hard put not to gasp at the wonder of the beacon.

The flinging fire leaped into the rocky mouth of the glen below me, where the horsemen passed in silence, scarcely deigning to look round. Large, heavy men, reckless how they bore their guns, or how they sat astride their horses, with leather jerkins and long boots and iron headgear and breastplates, plunder heaped, and flagons slung in front of them. More than thirty went along, like clouds upon red sunset. Some had carcases of sheep swinging with their skins on, others had deer and one had a child flung across his saddlebow. They had got the child, a very young one, for the sake of the dress, no doubt, which shone bright, where the light of the fire struck it, as if with gold and jewels. I longed in my heart to know most sadly what they would do with the little thing and whether it was alive or dead.

It touched me so to see that child, a prey among those vultures, that in my foolish rage I stood up and shouted to them, leaping on a rock, and heedless of my safety. Two of them turned round and one aimed his carbine at me, but the other said it was only a pixie and told him to save his powder. Little they knew, and less thought I, that the pixie then before them would dance their castle down one day.

John came up to me now that the danger was over and told me that we were lucky to escape and that the Doones would get me sooner or later if I behaved in this way.

I answered nothing at all, except to be ashamed of myself, and soon we found Peggy and Smiler together on the homeward road and grazing where the grass was good. My father never came to meet us and all at once my heart went down. There was not even the lanthorn light on the peg besides the cow's house and nobody said, "Hold your noise!" to the dogs, or shouted, "Here our Jack is!"

Woe is me! I cannot tell. How I knew I know not now – only that I slunk away without a tear or thought of weeping and hid myself in a saw-pit. All I wanted was to hide and for none to tell me anything.

By and by, a noise came down, as of woman's weeping, and there my mother and sister were, choking and holding each other. Although they were my dearest loves, I could not bear to look at them, until they seemed to want my help and turned away that I might come.

Chapter III

My dear father had been killed by the Doones of Bag-worthy, while riding home from Porlock market, on the Saturday evening. With him were six brother farmers and they were jogging along, singing to keep up their courage, when suddenly a horseman stopped in the starlight full across them. My father's friends doffed their caps to the robber, for by dress and arms they knew him well and there was not one but pulled out his bag and gave him his money, but my father set his staff above his head and rode at the Doone.

With a twist of his horse, the wild man escaped the charge, although he must have been truly amazed that anyone should resist him. My father and Smiler were carried away with the speed of the onslaught and found themselves in the midst of a dozen men who seemed to come out of a turf-rick, some on horse and some on foot. My father fought lustily and being of great size and strength, and his blood well up, they had no easy job with him. He cracked three or four crowns, the rest of the men began to draw their horses away, and he thought that he was master and would tell his wife about it.

But a man beyond the range of his staff was crouching by the peat stack, with a long gun set to his shoulder, and he got poor father against the sky, and I cannot tell the rest of it. Smiler came home with blood upon his withers, and father was found in the morning dead on the moor, with his ivy-twisted cudgel lying broken under him. Now whether this were an honest fight, God judge between the Doones and me.

It was more of sorrow than surprise, being such days of violence, that mother knew herself a widow, and her children fatherless. Of children there were only three, none of us fit to be useful yet, only to comfort our mother and try to help her in her sad task of keeping the home without the support of the man she had loved. I, John Ridd, was the eldest and felt it a heavy thing on me. Next came sister Annie, with about two years between us, and then the little Eliza.

Now, before I got home and found my sad loss – and no boy ever loved his father better than I loved mine – mother had done a most wondrous thing which made all the neighbours say she must at least be mad.

Upon the Monday morning, while her husband lay unburied, she cast a white hood over her hair, and gathered a black cloak round her, and taking council of no one, set off on foot for the Doone-gate.

In the early afternoon she came to the hollow and barren entrance, where in truth there was no gate, only darkness to go through. No gun was fired at her, only her eyes were covered over, and somebody led her by the hand, without any wish to hurt her. She remembered a very rough road, at the end of which they uncovered her eyes and she could scarce believe them.

For she stood at the head of a deep green valley, carved out of the mountains in a perfect oval, with a fence of sheer rock standing round it, eighty feet or a hundred high, from whose brink black wooded hills swept up to the skyline. By her side a little river glided out from underground with a soft dark babble to meet the daylight, then growing brighter, lapsed away and fell into the valley. There, as it ran down the meadow, alders stood on either marge, and grass was blading out upon it, and yellow tufts of rushes gathered, looking at the hurry. But further down, on either bank, were covered houses built of wood and stone, square and roughly cornered, set as if the brook were meant to be the street between them. Only one room high they were, and not placed opposite each other, but in and out as skittles are, but the first of all, which proved to be the captain's, was a sort of double house, or rather two houses joined together by a plank-bridge over the river. Fourteen cottages my mother counted, all very much of a pattern, and nothing to choose between them unless it were the captain's. Simple, innocent homes they looked, yet not a single house stood there but was the home of murder.

Two men led my mother down a steep stair, like the ladder of a hay-mow, and from there as far as the house of the captain and there they left her trembling and with tears in her eyes but determined to speak her mind.

A tall old man, Sir Ensor Doone, came out with a bill-hook in his hand, and hedger's gloves going up his arms, as if he were no better than a labourer at ditch-work. Only in his mouth and eyes, the way he moved and stood, and most of all his voice, even a child could know and feel that here was no ditch-labourer.

17

With his white locks moving upon his coat, he stopped and looked down at my mother, and she could not help herself but curtsey under his fixed black gazing.

"Good woman, you are none of us. What do you want?" He stood there scowling at my mother and in a flash, she replied, "Traitors! cut-throats! cowards! I am here to ask for my husband."

"Madam," said Sir Ensor Doone, "I crave pardon of you. I thought you were here for no good purpose. If we have your husband prisoner, he shall go free without ransom because I have insulted you."

"Sir," said my mother, being suddenly taken away with sorrow, because of his gracious manner, "please to let me cry a bit."

He stood away and by the way she cried, he knew that they had killed her husband. Then, having felt of grief himself, he was not angry with her but left her to begin again.

"Sir," said my mother, crying into her new red handkerchief, "I would not accuse anyone unfairly, but I have lost the very best husband God ever gave to a woman and it was done by the Doones."

"This matter must be seen to. It must be seen to at once," the old man answered. "Madam, if any wrong has been done, trust the honour of a Doone, I will redress it to my utmost. Come inside and rest yourself, while I ask about it. What was your good husband's name, and when and where fell this mishap?"

He placed a chair for her and my mother related her story as it had been told to her by the farmers who had ridden with my father on that fearful night.

"Madam, this is a serious thing," said Sir Ensor Doone graciously and showing grave concern. "My boys are a little wild, I know. And yet I cannot think that they would willingly harm anyone. And yet – and yet, you do look sad. Send Counsellor to me," he shouted from the door of his house; and down the valley went the call, "send Counsellor to Captain."

Counsellor Doone came in. He was a square-built man of enormous strength but not as tall as the rest of the Doones and his long grey beard reached to the leather of his belt. Great eyebrows overhung his face, like ivy on a pollard oak and under them two large brown eyes. And he had a power of hiding his eyes or showing them bright like a blazing fire. He stood there with his beaver hat off as Sir Ensor Doone spoke to him.

"Counsellor, this lady's worthy husband was slain, it seems, upon his return from the market at Porlock, no longer ago than last Saturday night."

"What was his name?" said the Counsellor with his eyes rolling inwards.

"Master John Ridd, as I understand. Counsellor, we have heard of him often, a worthy man and a peaceful one who meddled not with our duties. Now, if any of our boys have been rough, they shall answer for it dearly. What have you to say?"

"Oh sir," cried my mother, "tell the truth. Tell me who killed him."

The square man with the long grey beard, quite unmoved by my mother's plea, drew back to the door and spoke, and his voice was like a fall of stones at the bottom of a mine.

"A few words will be enough for this. Four or five of our best-behaved and most peaceful gentlemen went to the little market at Porlock with a sum of money. They bought some household stores and comforts at a very high price and set out again upon the homeward way. When they drew bridle to rest their horses, in the shelter of a

19

peat-rick, the night being very dark, a robber of great size and strength rode into the midst of them, thinking to kill or terrify. He had smitten three of them senseless and the last man tried to ward his blow with a pistol. Carver, sir, it was our brave and noble Carver, who saved the lives of all of them and glad enough they were to escape. Nevertheless, they hoped the robber had only received a flesh wound and would live to repent his sins."

As this atrocious tale of lies unfolded, mother was too much amazed to do any more than look at him, as if the earth must open. But the only thing that opened was the great brown eyes of the Counsellor, which rested on my mother's face with a dew of sorrow, as he spoke of sins.

She, unable to bear them, turned suddenly to Sir Ensor, and caught (as she fancied) a smile on his lips and a sense of quiet enjoyment.

"All the Doones are gentlemen," said the old man gravely, and looking as if he had never smiled since he was a baby. "We are always glad to explain, Madam, any mistake the country people may make about us and we wish you to understand that we will not charge your poor husband with robbery nor bring a suit at law to have his property and land taken away from his family."

My mother's head went round so, that she curtseyed to Sir Ensor, scarcely knowing where she was, but calling to mind her manners. All the time she felt a warmth, as if the right was with her, and yet she could not see her way to defend it before them. She dried her tears in haste, and went into the cold air, for fear of what she might say.

But when she was on the homeward road, and the sentinels had charge of her, blinding her eyes, as if she were not blind enough with weeping, someone came in haste behind her and thrust a heavy leather bag into the limp weight of her hand.

"Captain sends you this," he whispered. "Take it to the little ones."

But mother let it fall in a heap and fell on her knees before God so that even the Doones should pity her.

Chapter IV

Good folk, who dwell in a lawful land, may judge our neighbourhood harshly unless the whole truth is set before them and the story told of how the robbers came in the midst of us.

In or about the year of Our Lord 1640, when all the troubles of England were coming to a head, great estates in the north country were suddenly confiscated through some feud among families and strong influence at Court, and the landowners were turned upon the world, and might think themselves lucky to save their necks. One of these landowners was Sir Ensor Doone who was in dispute over his property with a cousin Lord Lorne. He had done no wrong, but suddenly found himself dispossessed and a beggar. Some say that, in the bitterness of that wrong and outrage, he slew a gentleman of the Court whom he supposed to have had a hand in the plundering of his fortunes. Others say that he went to King Charles I himself and raged at him in a manner beyond forgiveness. One thing, at any rate, is sure. He was made a criminal outlaw because of some violent deed he had performed following the unjust deprival of his possessions. He had a wife and sons and sought help from those whom he had helped, but beyond advice, he received nothing and this, it may be, tore at his heart more than the loss of land and fame.

In great despair Sir Ensor Doone resolved to settle in some other part of the country where nobody would know him and so, in an evil day for us, he brought his family to the West of England. Our country, which I love, is rugged and large and desolate. He found a place which almost seemed made for him, since it was isolated, easy to defend and difficult for others to get into.

Some of the country folk around brought him little offerings – a side of bacon, a keg of cider, joints of mutton or a brisket of venison, so that for a while he was very honest. But when the newness of his coming began to wear away, our good folk began to say that even gentlemen should do some work or pay others to do it and that it was unfair for them to take possession of such a fertile valley and do nothing to cultivate it. Instead of working, the young Doones grew up as robbers and took by force anything they wanted.

There was not more than a dozen of them, counting a few servants who had remained loyal to Sir Ensor, but soon they grew and multiplied in a manner surprising to think of, and it is true to say that the Doones increased much faster than their honesty. At first they brought some ladies with them and then, as time went on, they increased their numbers by carrying. They carried off many good farmers' daughters who were sadly displeased at first, but took to them kindly after a while and settled down and had babies. The Doones grew up big and powerful and did as they liked. They robbed and killed and took a fearful revenge if anyone struck one of them, so that people greatly feared them and let them alone. Their only virtue was loyalty to each other as a family and this led them into terrible deeds of violence from time to time.

You will understand when I tell you that our justices feared to hold any inquiry about my father's death. They would all have had to ride home at night and who could tell what might happen to them?

So we buried him quietly in the sloping little churchyard of Oare, as simple a place as could be, with the Lynn brook down below it. Annie was not allowed to come, because she cried so terribly, but she ran to the window, and saw it all, mooing there like a little calf, so frightened and so left alone. As for Eliza, she came with me, one on each side of mother, and not a tear was in her eyes, but for all that – poor little thing – she guessed what it is to lose a father.

Chapter V

About the rest of all that winter I remember very little, being only a young boy then, and missing my father most outdoors as when he took me on a shooting trip or training a new sheepdog. Sometimes when John Fry was shooting rats with father's gun, he would let me practise with it and gradually I won such skill that I sent nearly all the lead gutter from the north porch of our little church through our best barn door, a thing I have been sorry for since especially since I became churchwarden and has made me pardon many bad boys, but father was not buried on that side of the church.

But all this time while I was roving the hills, or about the farm, and even listening to John Fry, my mother being so much older, and feeling trouble longer, went about inside the house, or among the maids and fowls, not caring to talk to them, except when she broke out sometimes about the good master they had lost, all and every one of us. When Annie cried, it was quietly when nobody was around. She did not want to be seen and tried to keep her weeping to herself. Many times I caught her, and many times she turned to me, and then I could not look at her, but asked how long to dinner time. Annie was the love and joy of our cook Betty Muxworthy who had been with us for forty years. She would do anything for Annie and in truth everyone was taken with Annie at the very first time of seeing her. She had such pretty ways and manners, and such a look of kindness, and a sweet soft light in her blue eyes, full of trustful gladness. Everybody who looked at her seemed to grow the better for it because she knew no evil. And then the turn she had for cooking, you never would have expected it, and how it was her richest mirth to see that she had pleased you. I have never seen Annie's equal for making a weary man comfortable.

Almost everybody knows, in our part of the world at least, how pleasant and soft the fall of the land is round about Plover's Barrows farm. All about is strong dark mountain, spread with heath and desolate, but near our house, the valleys run down and there is open warmth and shelter. Here are trees and bright green grass and orchards full of contentment and one can hardly see the brook but one can hear it always. And indeed a stout good piece of it comes through our farmyard, and swells sometimes to a rush of waves, when the clouds are on the hill-tops. But all below where the valley bends there are pretty meadows and the sun spreads on the water. And nearly all of this is ours.

But about two miles below our farm, the Bagworthy water runs into the Lynn, and makes a real river of it. Thence it hurries away, with strength and a force of wilful waters, under the foot of a barefaced hill, and so to rocks and woods again, where the stream is covered over, and dark heavy pools delay it. There are plenty of fish down this way, and the further you go the bigger they are, having deeper grounds to feed in, and sometimes in the summer months, when mother could spare me off the farm, I came down here with Annie to help and caught almost a basketful of little trout and minnows with a hook and a bit of worm on it, but it so happened that we had never been up the Bagworthy water. We knew that it brought a good stream down, as full of fish as of pebbles, but perhaps we were afraid, for Bagworthy water ran out of Doone valley, a mile or so from the mouth of it.

But when I was turned fourteen years old, and put into good breeches, buckled at the knee, and strong blue worsted hose, knitted by my mother, it happened to me without choice, I may say, to explore the Bagworthy water. And this is how it came about.

My mother had long been ailing, and not able to eat much and we were all worried about it. Now I chanced to remember that once, at the time of the holidays, I had brought dear mother from Tiverton a jar of pickled loaches – small freshwater fish – caught by myself in the Lowman river, and baked in the kitchen oven with vinegar, a few leaves of bay and about a dozen peppercorns. And mother had said that, in all her life, she had never tasted anything fit to be compared with them. I resolved to get some loaches for her, and do them in the same way as before, just to make her eat a bit.

I set forth without a word to anyone, in the forenoon of St Valentine's day, 1675–76, I think it must have been. I did not ask Annie to come with me because the water was too cold, for the winter had been long, and snow lay here and there, in patches in the hollow of the banks, like a lady's gloves forgotten. And yet the spring was breaking forth, as it always does in Devonshire, when the turn of the days is over and although there was little to see of it, the air was full of feeling.

I shall never forget that day and how bitter cold the water was. I had left my coat at home and tied my shirt-sleeves back to my shoulders. Then I took off my shoes and hose and put them into a bag around my neck, and, taking a three-pronged fork firmly bound to a rod with cord, and a piece of canvas kerchief with a lump of bread inside it, I went into the pebbly water, trying to think how warm it was. For more than a mile all down the Lynn stream, scarcely a stone I left unturned, being thoroughly skilled in the tricks of the loach, and knowing how he hides himself. When I had travelled two miles or so, conquered now and then with cold, and coming out to rub my legs into a lively friction, and only fishing here and there because of the tumbling water, suddenly in an open space, where meadows spread about it, I found a good stream flowing softly into the body of our brook. And it brought, so far as I could guess by the sweep of it under my knee caps, a larger power of clear water than the Lynn itself had, only it came more quietly down, not being troubled with stairs and steps as the Lynn is, but gliding smoothly and forcibly, as if upon some set purpose. I climbed on to the bank and thought I would have something to eat. Now all the turn of my life hung upon that moment. But as I sat there munching a crust of Betty Muxworthy's sweet brown bread, and a bit of cold bacon along with it, and kicking my red heels against the dry earth to keep them warm, I knew that I must make a decision. It seemed a sad business now to go back and tell Annie there were no loaches, and yet it was a frightful thing, knowing what I did of it, to venture, where no man dared, up the Bagworthy water and I was only a boy.

However, as I ate more and more, my spirit arose within

me, and I thought what my father had been, and how he had told me a hundred times, never to be a coward. And then I felt ashamed of my faint heart, and I said to myself, "Now if father looks, he shall see that I obey him". So I put the bag round my neck again, and buckled my breeches far up from the knee, expecting deeper water, and crossing the Lynn went stoutly up under the branches which hang so dark on the Bagworthy river.

I found it strongly over-woven, turned and torn with thicket-wood, but not so rocky as the Lynn, and more inclined to go evenly.

Although often frightened by the deep, dark places and feeling that every step I took might never be taken backward, on the whole I had very good sport of loaches, trout and minnows, forking some, and tickling some, and driving others to shallow nooks, from where I could bail them ashore. Now, if you have ever been fishing, you will not wonder that I was led on, forgetting all about danger, and taking no heed of the time, but shouting in a childish way, whenever I caught a "whacker" as we called them at school in Tiverton, but in answer to all my shouts, there was never any sound at all, except of a rocky echo, or a scared bird hustling away, or the sudden dive of a water-vole, and the place grew thicker and thicker, and the covert grew darker above me, until I thought that the fishes might have a good chance of eating me, instead of my eating the fishes.

For now the day was falling fast behind the brown of the hill-tops, and the trees, being bare of leaves and hard, seemed giants ready to beat me. And every moment, as the sky was clearing up for a white frost, the cold of the water got worse and worse, until I was ready to cry with it. And so, in a sorry plight, I came to an opening in the bushes, where a great black pool lay in front of me, whitened with snow (as I thought) at the sides, till I saw it was only foam-froth.

Now, though I could swim with great ease and comfort, and feared no depth of water, yet I had no desire to go head over ears into this great pool, being so cramped and weary and cold, though wet only up to the middle, not counting my arms and shoulders. And the look of this black pit was enough to stop one from diving into it, so that I shuddered and drew back, not alone at the pool itself, and the black air there was about it, but also at the whirling manner, and wisping of white threads upon it in stripy circles round and round; and the centre still as jet.

But soon I saw the reason for the stir and depth of that great pit, as well as of the roaring sound which long had made me wonder. For skirting round one side, with great difficulty, because the rocks were high and steep, and the ledge at the foot so narrow, I came to a sudden sight and marvel, such as I never dreamed of. I found myself standing at the foot of a long pale slide of water, coming smoothly to me without a break, for a hundred yards or more, and fenced on either side with cliff, sheer and straight, and shining. The water came down in an even slope and looked like a plank of deal laid down a deep black staircase. However, there was no side-rail, nor any place to walk upon, only the channel a fathom wide, and the perpendicular walls of craggy rock, shutting out the evening.

The look of this place made me very scared, and I felt that I would give anything to be at home again with Annie cooking my supper and our dog Watch sniffing upward. Nevertheless there was nearly as much danger in going back as in going on and I thought it was worth the risk to find out what made the water come down like that, and what there was at the top of it.

I hitched the bag of fish around my neck more tightly, and not stopping to look much, for fear of fear, crawled along over the rocks, where the water had scooped the stone out and softly let my feet into the dip and rush of the torrent.

This was nearly the end of me, for the green waves came down with great force and knocked my legs from under me and I hit my head badly against a rock. I thought that I must die, but my fishing fork, praise God, stuck fast in the rock and I was carried up upon it. I was dizzy and deafened by the roar of the water, but presently the dash of it upon my face revived me and I thought that I had a chance.

I gathered my legs back slowly and won a foothold with the ashen stake set behind me and I saw that no choice was left me now, except that I must climb somehow up that hill of water, or else be washed down into the pool, and whirl around till it drowned me. There was no chance of going back by the way I had gone down into it, so I said the Lord's Prayer and, grasping my good loach-stick, steadied myself with my left hand, and began my course up the fearful torrent-way. To me it seemed half a mile at least of sliding water above me, but in truth it was little more than a furlong, as I came to know afterwards.

It would have been a hard ascent, even without the slippery slime, but the water was only about six inches deep and here and there I found a resting-place where I could hold on to the cliff and get my breath. And gradually as I went on, a warmth of courage breathed in me, to think perhaps that no one had dared to make that climb before me, and to wonder what my mother would say about it. And then I thought of my father also, and the pain in my feet became easier to bear.

Then at last I was near the top and the light was coming upon me, and I fought towards it; then suddenly I felt fresh air, and fell into it headlong.

Chapter VI

When I came to myself again, my hands were full of young grass and earth, and a little girl kneeling at my side was rubbing my forehead tenderly, with a dock-leaf and a handkerchief.

"Oh, I am so glad," she whispered softly, as I opened my eyes and looked at her, "now you will try to be better, won't you?"

I had never heard so sweet a sound as came from between her bright red lips, while there she knelt and gazed at me; neither had I ever seen anything so beautiful as the large dark eyes gazing down upon me, full of pity and wonder.

I sat upright with my fishing stick still in one hand and did not quite know what to say.

"What is your name?" she said, "and how did you come here, and what are these wet things in this great bag?"

"You had better let them alone," I said. "They are

loaches, for my mother. But I will give you some, if you like."

"Your feet are bleeding and you have no shoes or stockings. Is your mother very poor, poor boy?"

"No," I said, quite annoyed, "we are rich enough to buy all this great meadow, if we chose, and here are my shoes and stockings."

"And they are as wet as your poor torn feet. What is your name?"

"My name is John Ridd. What is yours?"

"Lorna Doone," she answered in a low voice, as if afraid of it, and hanging her head, so that I could see only her forehead and eyelashes. "If you please, my name is Lorna Doone, and I thought you must have known it."

Then I stood up and touched her hand, and tried to make her look at me, but she only turned away the more. Young and harmless as she was, her name seemed to make her guilty. She started to cry.

"Don't cry," I said, "I am sure you have never done any harm. I will give you all my fish, Lorna, and catch some more for mother; only don't turn away from me."

She flung her little soft arms up, in the passion of her tears, and looked at me so piteously, that what did I do but kiss her. She gave me no encouragement, but wiped her lips and drew away from me as if I had taken a liberty. Then I felt my cheeks grow burning red and I was sorry, for I was only a farmer's son and she was born a lady.

Seeing how I felt, and knowing that I had kissed her, although she was such a little girl, only about eight years old, she turned to the stream in a bashful manner, and began to watch the water, and rubbed one leg against the other.

I, for my part, being hurt at her behaviour to me, took up all my things to go, and made a fuss about it to let her know I was going. But she did not call me back at all, as I had made sure she would do. I knew that I had to go down into the water again and that it was almost certain death to me. It looked as dark as pitch, and so at the mouth I turned round again, and came back to her and said, "Lorna."

"Oh, I thought you had gone," she answered. "Why did you ever come here? Do you know what they would do to us, if they found you here with me?"

"Beat us, I daresay, very hard, or me at least. They could never beat you."

"No, they would kill us both outright, and bury us here by the water, and the water often tells me that I must come to that."

"But what should they kill me for?"

"Because you have found the way up here and that is unbelievable. Please go, John. I like you very much and when your feet are well, you can come and tell me how they are."

"Lorna, I like you very much indeed and I never saw anyone like you.

"I must come back again tomorrow and so must you to see me. Our dog has just had puppies and when it can leave its mother, I will bring you one."

"Oh dear, they won't let me have a dog. They say they are such noisy things."

"Only put your hand in mine and I will bring you the loveliest puppy."

"Hush!" A shout came down the valley and my heart trembled. Lorna's face was changed to a look of terror. She clung to me and I at once made up my mind to save her or to die with her. She took courage from me and put her cheek quite close to mine.

"Come with me down the waterfall. I can carry you easily, and mother will take care of you."

"No," cried Lorna, "I will tell you what to do. They are only looking for me. You see that hole, that hole there?"

She pointed to a little niche in the rock, which was at the end of the meadow, about fifty yards away from us. In the fading of the twilight, I could just see it.

"Yes, I see it, but they will see me crossing the grass to get there."

"There is a way out from the top of it. They would kill me for telling you. Oh, here they come. I can see them."

Lorna turned white and began to sob, but I pulled her behind some bushes and close down to the water where it was quiet and shelved down deeply before it came to the lip of the chasm. Here they could not see either of us from the upper valley and luckily I had picked up my fish and taken my fishing fork away.

Hidden in that hollow nest, we saw a dozen fierce men come down on the other side of the water, not bearing any fire-arms, but looking relaxed and jovial as if they had come from riding and had just eaten a good dinner. "Queen, queen!" they were shouting, "where the pest has our little queen gone?"

"They always call me 'Queen', and I am to be queen by and by," Lorna whispered to me with her soft cheek on my rough one. "Oh look, they are crossing by the trees there, and then they are sure to see us."

"Stop," I said, "I see what to do. I must get into the water and you must pretend to be asleep."

"Yes, yes, over in the meadow there. But how bitter cold it will be for you!" She saw in a moment the way to do it and crept away into the grass while I stepped into the water and lay down in it, with my head between two blocks of stone and the flood coming over me. From time to time I caught a glimpse of Lorna whose beauty and whose kindness had made me yearn to be with her. She

35

was lying on the grass beneath a rock, thirty or forty yards from me, pretending to be fast asleep, with her dress spread out beautifully and her hair drawn over her.

Presently one of the great rough men came round a corner and found her. He caught her up in his arms, and kissed her so that I heard him, and if I had only brought my gun, I would have tried to shoot him.

"Here's our queen, here's the captain's daughter!" he shouted to his comrades, "fast asleep by God and hearty! I shall bring her, and you, back to your drinking – all of you!"

He set her dainty little form upon his great square shoulder, and her small feet in one broad hand, and so in triumph marched away. Going up that darkened glen, little Lorna turned and put up a hand to me, and I put up a hand to her, in the thick of the mist and the willows.

I crept into a bush for warmth, for I was cold and hungry by now and I thought of home. Then, as daylight sank, I knew that now must be my time to get away, if indeed that were possible. Therefore, wringing the water from my sodden breeches, I managed to crawl from the bank to the niche in the cliff, which Lorna had shown me. I entered and held on by some dead fern stems and did hope that no one would shoot me. I felt myself going down a deep passage into a pit of darkness. It was no good to catch the sides, for the whole thing seemed to go with me. Then, without knowing how, I was leaning over a dark sheet of water.

This water was of black radiance, as are certain diamonds, spanned across with vaults of rock. It sent back no reflection and appeared to be bottomless and without sides or ending. Chilled and full of dread I ventured on, knowing that I could slip and go to the bottom, if there were one.

But suddenly a robin sang (as they will do after dark,

towards spring) in the brown fern and ivy behind me. I took it for our little Annie's voice (for she could call any robin), and gathering quick warm comfort, sprang up the steep way towards the starlight. Climbing back over the sloping stones, I heard the cold greedy wave go lapping like a blind black dog, into the distance of arches, and hollow depths of darkness.

Chapter VII

I can assure you, and tell no lie (as John Fry always used to say, when telling his very largest), that I scrambled back to the mouth of that pit, as if the evil one had been after me and sat down in the little opening, which Lorna had pointed out to me, and wondered whether she had meant me to run down into the pit and be drowned, and give no more trouble. But in less than half a minute, I was ashamed of that idea. Lorna would not send me to my death, and I thought what she said must be quite true about the way out of this horrible place.

I began to search around, although my teeth were chattering, and all my bones beginning to ache, with the chilliness and the wetness. Before very long the moon appeared over the edge of the mountain, and among the trees at the top of it, and then I saw rough, rocky steps made as if with a sledgehammer, narrow, steep and far apart, scooped here and there in the side of the entrance, and then round a bulge of the cliff, like the marks upon a great brown loaf, where a hungry child has picked at it. And higher up, where the light of the moon shone broader upon the precipice, there seemed to be a rough broken track, like the shadow of a crooked stick thrown upon a house-wall.

I was not much encouraged by this, but I put my trust in God and decided to have a try, especially since I saw a movement of lights at the head of the valley as if lanterns were coming after me, and that settled it.

Straightway I set foot on the lowest step and clung to the rock with my nails and prepared to jump on to the second step. I managed that too with the aid of my stick, but the third step was the hardest of all for the rock swelled out over me and I could not see how I could reach it. Then I saw a good stout rope hanging in a groove of shadow, and just managed to reach the end of it.

How I climbed up and across the clearing, and found my way home through the Bagworthy forest is more than I can remember now, for I was so weary that all the rest of it seemed a dream.

When I got home, all the supper was in, and the men sitting at the white table, and mother and Annie and Lizzie nearby, all eager and offering to begin (except, indeed, my mother, who was looking out of the doorway), and by the fire was Betty Muxworthy, scolding, and cooking, and tasting her work, all in a breath, as one might say. I looked through the door from the dark by the woodstack, and was half of a mind to stay out, like a dog, for fear of the scolding and possible punishment, but the way my dear mother was looking about, and the browning of the sausages got the better of me.

But nobody could get out of me where I had spent all the day and evening, although they worried me never so much, and longed to shake me to pieces, especially Betty

Muxworthy, who could never learn to let well alone.

How the year went by, I know not. I was out all day, shooting or fishing, or minding the farm, or riding to look for a stray animal or away by the seaside below Glenthorne, wondering at the great waters and resolving, as many boys have done, to go for a sailor. I had been in a boat nearly twice, but the second time mother found it out, and came and drew me back again, and after that she cried so badly, that I was forced to give my word to her, to go no more without telling her.

The fright I had taken that night in Glen Doone satisfied me for a long time afterwards, and I took good care not to venture even in the fields and woods of the outer farm without John Fry for company. John was greatly surprised and pleased at the value I now set on him, until what between the desire to boast, and the longing to talk things over, I gradually told him all that had happened to me, except, indeed, about Lorna, whom a sort of shyness kept me from mentioning although I thought of her and wished very often to see her again. But I was only a boy as yet and naturally inclined to seek the company of other boys, not little girls.

Chapter VIII

It happened upon a November evening (when I was about fifteen years old, and out-growing my strength very rapidly, my sister Annie being turned thirteen, and a deal of rain having fallen, and all the troughs in the yard being flooded), that the ducks in the court made a terrible quacking, instead of marching off to their pen, one behind another. Thereupon Annie and I ran out, to see what might be the matter. There were thirteen ducks, ten white ones and three striped and they all quacked very movingly. They pushed their gold-coloured bills here and there, and they jumped on the triangles of their feet, and sounded out of their nostrils, and some of the over-excited ones ran along low on the ground, quacking grievously, with their bills snapping and bending, and the roof of their mouths showing.

Annie began to cry, "dilly, dilly, einy, einy, ducksey," to a tune they seem to have accepted as the national duck's

41

anthem, but instead of being soothed by it, they only quacked three times as hard, and ran round till we were giddy. And then they shook their tails all together, and looked grave, and went round and round again. We knew at once that something had gone seriously wrong in the duck-world and, like a good duck-wife, Annie counted them and could only see thirteen of them when there should have been fourteen.

And so we began to search about and the ducks ran to lead us and when we got down to the foot of the courtyard where the two great ash trees stand by the side of the little water, we saw that the old white drake, the father of all, was in bad trouble though still quacking bravely. The brook was coming down in a great brown flood and this was enough to frighten him, but also a hurdle which was usually stretched just above the water to keep our animals in and those of the neighbouring farmer out, had come down and the drake's shoulder was jammed between two bars of it.

The hurdle rose and fell with the water and he went with it with his top-knot full of water, unable to understand it and his tail washed away from him. There was small doubt but that he would drown very soon unless we could get to him.

Annie was crying and wringing her hands and I was about to rush into the water, although I did not like the look of it, but hoped to hold on by the hurdle, when a man on horseback came suddenly round the corner of the great ash-hedge on the other side of the stream, and his horse's feet were in the water.

"You there," he cried, "get back, boy. The flood will carry you down like a straw. I will do it for you, and no trouble."

With that he leaned forward, and spoke to his mare – she

was just of the tint of a strawberry, a young thing, very beautiful – and she arched up her neck, as disliking the job, yet, trusting him, would attempt it.

She entered the flood with her dainty fore-legs sloped further and further in front of her, and her delicate ears pricked forward, and the size of her great eyes increasing, but he kept her straight by the pressure of his knee on her. The water foamed up over her shoulders and she tossed up her lip and scorned it, for now her courage was waking. Then as the rush of it swept her away, and she struck with her fore-feet down the stream, he leaned from his saddle, in a manner which I never could have thought possible, and caught up Tom, the old drake, with his left-hand and set him before him and smiled at his faint quack of gratitude. In a moment all three were carried downstream, and the rider lay flat on his horse, and tossed the hurdle clear from him, and made for the bend of smooth water.

They landed some thirty or forty yards lower, in the midst of our kitchen garden where the winter cabbage was, but though Annie and I crept in through the hedge, and were full of thanks and admiring him, he would answer us never a word until he had spoken in full to the mare as if explaining the whole to her.

"Sweetheart, I know you could have leaped it," he said as he patted her cheek, being on the ground by this time, and she was nudging up to him with the water pattering off from her, "but I had good reason, Winnie dear, for making you go through it."

She answered him kindly with her soft eyes, and sniffed at him very lovingly, and they understood one another. Then he took from his waistcoat two peppercorns and made the old drake swallow them, and tried him softly upon his legs, where the leading gap in the hedge was. Old Tom stood up quite bravely, and flapped his wings and

43

shook off the wet from his tail feathers, and then away into the courtyard to see his family. They gathered round him, making a noise in their throats and put their bills together to thank God for this great deliverance.

Having taken all this trouble and watched the end of that adventure, the gentleman turned round to us with a pleasant smile on his face as if he were lightly amused with himself, and we came up and looked at him. He was rather short, about John Fry's height or maybe a little taller, but very strongly built and springy, although his legs were bowed with much riding and he looked as if he lived on horseback. To a boy like me he seemed very old, being over twenty and having a well-grown beard, but he was not more than four-and-twenty, fresh and ruddy-looking with a short nose and keen blue eyes and a merry way about him. Yet he had a sharp, stern way like the crack of a pistol if he was annoyed and we knew (for children see such things) that it was safer to tickle than tackle him.

"Well, young 'uns, what are you gaping at?" He gave pretty Annie a chuck under the chin and looked me over.

"Your mare," said I. "I never saw such a beauty, sir. Will you let me have a ride on her?"

He looked at me with a dry little whistle, and thrust his hands into his breeches pockets and grinned but said nothing.

"Good sir, only trust me with her, and I will not over-ride her."

"That is for sure, my son. She is more likely to over-ride you. But come, let us go up to the house. I am your mother's cousin, boy. Tom Faggus is my name, as every-one knows, and this is my young mare, Winnie."

What a fool I must have been not to know it at once! Tom Faggus, the great highwayman, and his young strawberry mare. Already her fame was noised abroad, nearly as much as her master's and I longed more than ever to ride her, though there was some fear at the back of it for there was a rumour that she was really a witch.

"Cousin Sarah," said Tom Faggus, as my mother came curious out of the house, "I shall not stay but glad I am to see your fine boy and girl and here is another." He picked up Lizzie who had followed my mother out of the house.

"Cousin Tom," said mother, "it would be a sad thing if you did not stay. We cannot entertain you as the lordly inns on the road do, and we have but simple food. But the men will go home being Saturday and so you will have the fireside all to yourself and the children. There are some collops of red deer flesh and a ham just down from the chimney, and some dried salmon from Lynmouth weir and cold roast pig and some oysters. And if none of those are to your liking, we could roast two woodcocks in half an hour, and Annie would make the toast for them. And the good folk made some mistake last week, going up the country, and left a keg of old Holland cordial inside the wood-rick, having borrowed our Smiler without asking leave. John Fry would have taken it, but for our Jack. Our Jack was a little too sharp for him."

So Tom Faggus stopped to sup with us that night and took a little of everything finishing up with a woodcock on toast and the cordial with some hot water. And having changed his wet things first, he seemed to be in fair appetite, and praised Annie's cooking mightily, with a relishing noise like a smack of his lips, and a rubbing of his hands together, whenever he could spare them.

He had got John Fry's best clothes on, for he said he was not good enough to wear my father's (which mother kept to look at), and in truth she was very glad that he refused when I offered them. But John Fry was proud to have it in his power to say that such a famous man had ever dwelt in any clothes of his, and afterwards he made show of them. For Mr Faggus' glory then, thought not so great as now it is, was spreading very fast indeed all about our neighbourhood, and even as far as Bridgewater.

Tom Faggus was a jovial soul if ever there has been one, not caring to seek evil although he was a highwayman. There was about him such a genuine love of human nature, that if a traveller said a good thing, he would give him back his purse again, but still he did take people's money and the law was bitterly against him.

I did not understand much of this at the time, but observed that mother seemed frightened, and whispered to him now and then, not to talk of this or that, because of the children being there. Then he always nodded with a wise expression and drank some more of the cordial.

"Now let us go and see Winnie, Jack," he said to me after supper. "For the most part I feed her before myself, but she was pretty hot when we got here. Now she must be grieving for me, and I never let her grieve long."

I was glad to go with him, and Annie came slyly after us. The filly was walking to and fro on the bare floor of the stable (for he would not let her have any straw until he could make a bed for her), and without so much as a headstall on, for he would not have her fastened. "Do you take my mare for a dog?" he had said, when John Fry brought him a halter. And now she ran to him like a child, and her great eyes shone at the stable lantern.

"Hit me, Jack, and see what she will do. I will not let her hurt you." He was rubbing her ears all the time he spoke, and she was leaning against him. Then I pretended to strike him, and in a moment she caught me by the waistband and lifted me clean from the ground, and was casting me down to trample upon me, when he stopped her suddenly.

"What think you of that, boy? Have you horse or dog that would do that for you? And she will do more than that. If I were to whistle by and by in the tone that tells her I'm in danger, she would break the stable door down and rush into the room to me. Nothing will keep her from me then, stone wall or church tower. Ah, Winnie, Winnie, you little witch, we shall die together." Then he fed her and watched her eat every morsel with two or three drinks of pure water ministered between whiles, and then he made her bed in a form I had never seen before, and so we said goodnight to her.

Afterwards he kept us very merry, sitting in the great chimney corner, and making us play games with him. After that he told us whole pages of stories speaking with the voices of twenty people, giving each person the proper manner, and the proper place to speak from, so that Annie and Lizzie ran all about and searched the clock and the linen press. And he changed his face every moment so, and with such mimicry, that without so much as a smile of his own, he made even mother laugh so that she broke her new tenpenny waistband, and as for us children, we rolled on the floor, and Betty Muxworthy roared in the scullery.

47

Chapter IX

Now although Mr Faggus was so clever and generous and celebrated, I am not sure, on the whole, whether we were rather proud of him as a member of our family, or inclined to be ashamed of him.

Tom Faggus had much cause to be harsh with the world, and yet all acknowledged him very pleasant when a man gave up his money. And often and often he paid the toll for the carriage he had robbed, because he had emptied the travellers' pockets and did not wish to add inconvenience. By trade he had been a blacksmith in the town of Northmolton in Devonshire, a rough type of place at the end of Exmoor. Tom Faggus could read and write and he had solid substance; a piece of land worth a hundred pounds and grazing rights on common land for two hundred sheep and twenty-five cattle. He had been left an orphan and began to work right early, becoming famous as a farrier and winning a gold cup for the best-shod horse in the north of Devon.

Within a month of his victory, when his trade was growing upon him and he was about to be married, he received a written order from a lawyer. This was the beginning of a lawsuit with Sir Robert Bampfylde, a gentleman of the neighbourhood, who tried to oust him from his common, and drove his cattle and harassed them. And by that lawsuit poor Tom was ruined altogether for Sir Robert was able to bribe witnesses and then all Tom's goods and his farm were sold up, and even his smithy taken. But he saddled his horse, before they could catch him, and rode away to Southmolton, looking more like a madman than a good farrier, as the people said who saw him. But when he arrived there, instead of comfort, they showed him the door for the news of his losses had gone before him, his sweetheart refused to marry him and within a month she married another man.

All this was very hard upon Tom and he became a highwayman being determined to treat the world as the world had treated him. He was popular with the people, especially the landlords whom he paid well; he would invite certain squires and noblemen to dine with him at inns where he was welcome and he gave plenty to charity.

One of his earliest meetings was with Sir Robert Bampfylde himself, who was riding along the road with only one serving man behind him. Tom Faggus put a pistol to his head, being then obliged to be violent until his reputation was made, while the serving-man pretended to be a long way round the corner. Sir Robert pulled out his purse, quite trembling in the hurry of his politeness. Tom took the purse and his ring and timepiece and then handed them back with a very low bow saying that it was against custom for one robber to rob another. Then he turned to the unfaithful servant and rebuked him severely for his cowardice, and stripped him of all his property.

Tom had never been guilty of bloodshed, he never robbed a poor man, nor insulted a woman and was very good to the Church. He was a patriotic man and full of jest and jollity. He and his famous young mare Winnie were popular, while everyone cursed the Doones.

So time went on, I grew to be a big man and I began to work at the farm in earnest. When I remembered Lorna Doone, it seemed no more than the thought of a dream which I could hardly call to mind.

Annie was now a fine girl, beautiful to behold, but our little Eliza, though full of wit which was sometimes uncomfortable for others, was small and skinny, the result of a fall which mother had before her baby was born.

As for the Doones, they were thriving still, and no one to come against them, except indeed by word of mouth, to which they paid no heed whatever. Complaints were made from time to time, both in high and low quarters, and once or twice in the highest of all, to wit, King Charles II himself. But His Majesty made a good joke about it and moreover the main authorities were a long way off; the Lord Chancellor had no cattle on Exmoor, and as for my lord the Chief Justice, some rogue had taken his silver spoons and he swore that he would never hang another man until he had that one by the neck. So the Doones did as they liked and the only man who would have dared to close quarters with them, Tom Faggus, was himself in trouble with the law. Moreover he had transferred his business to the neighbourhood of Wantage, in the county of Berks, where he found the climate drier, also good downs and commons excellent for galloping, and richer yeoman than ours and better roads to rob them on.

Chapter X

As I grew older I began to think of Lorna Doone, the little maid of so many years back, and wondered if she ever thought of me. I took to venturing into Doone country and one day found myself not half a mile away from their stronghold.

The ridge of highland on which I stood, curved to the right and left of me, keeping the same height and crowned with trees and brush-wood. At about half a mile in front of me, but looking as if I could throw a stone to strike any man upon it, another crest or ridge, just like the one on which I stood, bent round to meet it, but failed by reason of two narrow clefts, of which I could only see the brink. One of these clefts was the Doone-gate, with a portcullis of rock above it, and the other was the chasm, by which I had once made entrance. Between them, where the hills fell back, as in a perfect oval, traversed by the winding water, lay a bright green valley, rimmed with sheer black rock, and seeming to have sunken bodily from the bleak rough heights above. It looked as if no frost could enter, neither winds go ruffling: only spring, and hope, and comfort, breathe to one another. Even now the rays of sunshine dwelt, and fell back on themselves, whenever the clouds lifted; and the pale blue glimpse of the growing day seemed to find young encouragement.

Looking across, I could see the little opening in the cliff through which I had made my exit those seven years ago. No bigger than a rabbit hole it seemed from where I stood and yet of all the scene before me, that had the most attraction. Now gazing at it, with full thought of all that it had cost me, I saw a little figure come, and pause, and pass into it. Something very light and white, nimble, smooth and elegant, gone almost before I knew that anyone had been there. And yet my heart came to my ribs, and all my blood was in my face, and pride within me fought with shame, and vanity with self-contempt; for though seven years were gone, and I from boyhood come to manhood, and thinking she must have forgotten me as I had half forgotten her; at that moment once for all I felt that I was face to face with fate for better or worse with Lorna Doone.

Chapter XI

After some thought, I decided to make a visit to Glen
Doone, by way of the perilous passage discovered in my
boyhood. Therefore I waited for nothing more than the
slow arrival of new breeches, made by a good tailor at
Porlock, for I wanted to look my best; and when they
were come and approved, I started, regardless of the ex-
pense, and forgetting (like a fool) how badly they would
take the water. What with the urging of the tailor, and my
own misgivings, the time was now come round again to
the high day of St Valentine and I took this as a good
omen.

I chose a seven foot staff of ash, and fixed a loach-fork in
it, to look as I had looked before and out of the back door I
went, and so through the little orchard, and down the
brawling Lynn-brook. Not being now so much afraid, I
struck across the thicket land between the meeting waters,
and came upon the Bagworthy stream near the great black

whirlpool. Nothing amazed me so much as to find how shallow the stream now looked to me, although the pool was still as black and greedy as it used to be. And still the great rocky slide was dark and difficult to climb, though the water, which had come up to my knees, now only covered my ankles. After some effort, I reached the top and halted to look about me well, before trusting to broad daylight.

The winter had been a very mild one, and now the spring was on its way and bank and bush were touched with it. The valley into which I gazed was fair with early promise, having shelter from the wind, and taking all the sunshine.

While I was enjoying the sights and sounds of nature, a sweeter note than thrush or ouzel ever wooed a mate in, floated on the valley breeze, at the quiet turn of sundown. I kept myself in a black niche of the rock, where the fall of the water began, lest the sweet singer (seeing me) should be alarmed and flee away. But presently I ventured to look, using a bush as cover, and then I beheld the loveliest sight – one glimpse of which was enough to make me kneel in the coldest water.

By the side of the stream, she was coming to me, even among the primroses, as if she loved them all; and every flower looked the brighter as her eyes were on them. Her hair was flowing from a wreath of white violets, and the grace of her coming was like the appearance of the first windflower.

I came from the dark mouth of the chasm and stood, afraid to look at her. She was turning to fly, not knowing me, and frightened, when I fell on my knees on the grass, and I just said, "Lorna Doone!"

She knew me at once and a smile broke through her trembling, as sunshine comes through willow leaves.

Then she made a pretence of anger and cried, "Who are you, sir, and how do you know my name?"

"I am John Ridd," I answered, "the boy who gave you those beautiful fish, when you were only a little thing, seven years ago today."

"Yes, the poor boy who was frightened so, and obliged to hide here in the water."

"And do you remember how kind you were, and saved my life by your quickness, and went away riding upon a big man's shoulder, as if you had never seen me, and yet looked back through the willow trees?"

"Oh yes, I remember everything, but, Master Ridd, I think you cannot know what the dangers of this place are, and the nature of the people."

"Yes, I know about that and am frightened greatly, all the time when I do not look at you."

She did not answer me and I saw that she was trembling and guessed that it was for me.

"Mistress Lorna, I will go. Try to think of me now and then and I will bring you some new-laid eggs, for our young blue hen is just coming into lay."

"I thank you heartily," said Lorna, "but you need not come to see me. You can put them in my little bower, where I go to think and be away from *them*." And she smiled, with a light that made me want to cry out for no other way, only the way to her dear heart. So I touched her white hand softly, when she gave it to me, and made my way home, mad with any man in the world who would dare to think of looking at her.

Chapter XII

Spring came on, frosts were gone, the southwest wind blew softly, the lambs were at play with the daisies and it was more than I could do to keep from thought of Lorna. I stood beneath a great budding elm and carved L.D. upon it and wondered at the buds of thought which seemed to swell inside me.

As no Lorna came to me except in dreams or fancy, and as my life was not worth living without constant sign of her, forth I must go again to find her and tell her what was in my heart. This time I longed to take my gun, and was half resolved to do so, because it seemed so hard a thing to be shot at and have no chance of shooting, but when I came to remember the steepness, and the slippery nature of the waterslide, there seemed little likelihood of keeping my powder dry. Therefore I was armed with nothing but a good stout holly staff, seasoned well for many a winter in our back-kitchen chimney.

It was hard going before I reached the top of the rift leading into Doone glade, for the stream was rushing down in strength, and raving at every corner, tremendous rain having fallen the night before with no wind to scatter it. However, I reached the top before dark, with more difficulty than danger and sat down in a place which was comfortable for my back and legs. And there I was so pleased to be on dry land again and come to look for my Lorna and in such a beautiful place, that I fell asleep with my holly stick in front of me.

Suddenly my sleep was broken by a shade cast over me, between me and the low sunlight. Lorna Doone was standing there.

"Master Ridd, are you mad?" she said, and took my hand to move me.

"Not mad, but half asleep," I replied, hoping she would keep hold of me.

"Come away, come away, if you care for life. The patrol will be here directly. Be quick, Master Ridd, let me hide you."

"I will not stir a step", said I, though I was really quite frightened, "unless you call me John."

"Well, John, then, Master John Ridd. Be quick and follow me."

Without another word, she led me, though with many timid glances, towards the upper valley to her little bower where the inlet through the rock was. Inside the niche of stone was the stairway hewn from rock and leading up the mountain, by means of which I had escaped before. To the right side of this, was the mouth of the pit, still looking very formidable, though Lorna laughed at my fear of it, for she drew her water from there. But on the left was a narrow crevice, very difficult to see, for it had a curtain of grey ivy over it.

Lorna raised the screen for me, but I had a hard time getting through because of my height and size. At last I broke into the pleasant room, the lone retreat of Lorna.

The chamber was of unhewn rock, round as near as might be, eighteen or twenty feet across and decorated with a rich variety of growing fern and moss and lichen. Overhead there was no ceiling but the sky itself, flaked with little April clouds whitely wandering over it. The floor was made of soft, low grass mixed with moss and primroses, and in a niche of shelter moved the delicate wood-sorrel. Around the side were "chairs" of stone, and in the midst a tiny spring arose with crystal beads in it, and a soft voice as of a laughing dream, and dimples like a sleeping babe. Then, after going round a little, the water overflowed the edge and softly went through lines of light, to shadows and an underground stream.

While I was gazing around in wonder, Lorna turned to me lightly (as her manner was) and said, "Where are the new-laid eggs, Master Ridd? Or has the blue hen ceased laying?"

"Here are some," I answered. "I would have brought you twice as many, but I feared to crush them in the narrow ways, Mistress Lorna."

And so I laid out two dozen upon the moss of the rock ledge, unwinding the wisp of hay from each, as it came safe out of my pocket. Lorna looked with growing wonder, as I added one to one, and when I had placed them side by side, and asked her to count them, to my amazement what did she do but burst into a flood of tears!

"What have I done?" I asked, greatly disturbed, "oh what have I done to upset you so?"

"It is nothing done by you, Master Ridd," she answered very proudly, as if nothing I did could matter, "it is only something that comes upon me, with the scent of the pure, true clover-hay. Moreover, you have been too kind and I am not used to kindness."

I did not know what to say for fear of making things worse, and therefore looked at the floor and said nothing.

Presently she turned to me and said in the softest voice that ever flowed between two lips, "Master Ridd, have I done anything to offend you?"

It was all I could do not to catch her up and kiss her, but it struck me suddenly that this would be taking advantage of her trust and helplessness and I said, within my heart, "John Ridd, be on your very best manners with this lonely maiden."

Lorna seemed to feel that she could trust me and sitting beside me, told me her story which I shall now relate as she told it to me, in her own sweet voice and manner.

Chapter XIII

"I cannot go through all my thoughts, so as to make them clear to you," said Lorna. "I do not know where the beginning of my story lies, nor where the middle ought to be, nor even how at the present time I feel, or think, or ought to think. If I look for help to those around me, who should tell me right and wrong (being older and much wiser), I meet sometimes with laughter, and at other times with anger.

"There are but two in the world who ever listen and try to help me; one of them is my grandfather and the other is a man of wisdom whom we call the Counsellor. My grandfather, Sir Ensor Doone, is very old and harsh of manner (except indeed to me). He seems to know what is right and wrong, but not to want to think of it. The Counsellor, on the other hand, though very clever does not answer my questions or take me seriously and makes me feel he is laughing at me.

"Among the women, there is no one for me to talk to, since my Aunt Sabina died. She took such pains to teach me and was a learned and honourable lady who became more and more distressed by the coarseness, and the violence and the ignorance round her. I was her only comfort, and I am sure she was my only one, and, when she died, it was more to me than if I had lost a mother.

"I cannot remember my father or mother, although they say that my father was the eldest son of Sir Ensor Doone, and the bravest and the best of them. And so they call me heiress to this little realm of violence. I am their Princess or their Queen.

"You may think," continued Lorna, "that I should be happy in this beauteous valley, but all around me is violence and robbery. There is no one to lead me forward, there is no one to teach me right. Young as I am, I live beneath a curse that lasts for ever.

"Often I wonder at the odds of fortune which made me the heiress of this mad domain, this sanctuary of unholiness. It is not likely that I shall have much power or authority and yet the Counsellor is respectful to me as my Lord of the Treasury, and his son seeks my hand as if it were a Royal alliance. One privilege I have, requested rather than demanded, which is to have to myself this lower end of the valley. Therefore no one, apart from the sentries, ever trespasses on me here unless it be my grandfather, or the Counsellor, or Carver.

"By your face, Master Ridd, I see that you have heard of Carver Doone. He has strength and courage and wisdom as might well be expected from the son of the Counsellor, but he differs from his father in being very hot and savage and he is not to be opposed or contradicted.

"I have little to do with the women here except for Gwenny Carfax, my little maid. Her mother died and her father vanished and I found her starving on a peat-rick and brought her here. She interferes with nobody and is allowed by the men to wander where she will. Without her, I should be lonely indeed. If it were not for my grandfather, I should have taken Gwenny and fled from this valley long ago, but I cannot bear that he should die with no gentle hand to comfort him and I fear to think of the conflicts that could arise if I left and several men claimed the leadership."

Lorna's story was finished. She took my hand and bade me not return until a month had passed and this was for my safety.

What could I do but agree for she was near to tears? I went home in sorry spirits and was so greatly vexed with my own hesitation, stupidity or shyness, or whatever else it was, that I did not tell her what was in my heart which was that I must die unless she let me love her.

Chapter XIV

One day when work was over, I had seen to the horses, for now it was foolish to trust John Fry because he had so many children and his wife had taken to nagging, and just as I was saying to myself that in five days more my month would be done, and I would be free to seek Lorna, a man came riding up from the ford where the road goes through the Lynn stream. As soon as I saw that it was not Tom Faggus, I went no further to meet him, counting that it must be some traveller bound for Brendon or Cheriton, and likely enough he would come and beg for a draught of milk or cider and then go on again after asking the way.

But instead of that, he stopped at our gate, and stood up from his saddle and shouted, as if he were somebody, and all the time he was flourishing a white thing in the air like the bands our parson wears. So I crossed the courtyard to speak to him.

"Service of the King!" he said. "Come here, farmer, at

risk of fine and imprisonment."

Although not pleased with this, I went to him as became a loyal man. I did so at my leisure, however, for there is no man borne who can hurry me, though I hasten for any woman.

"Plover Barrows Farm!" said he. "God only knows how tired I am. Is there anywhere in this cursed county a cursed place called Plover Barrows Farm? For the last twenty mile at least they told me it were only half a mile further or just round the corner. Can you tell me where it is, great fellow?"

"Sir," I replied, "this is Plover's Barrows Farm and you are kindly welcome. There are sheep's kidneys for supper and bright ale. But why do you think so ill of us? We do not like to be cursed so."

"Nay, I think no ill," he said, "sheep's kidneys are good, uncommon good, if they do them without burning. But I have been riding ten days and never a decent meal." All this time he was riding across the straw of our courtyard, getting his weary legs out of the stirrup leathers, and so sore and stiff he was almost afraid to stand yet. A coarse-grained, hard-faced man he was, some forty years of age or so and of middle height and stature. He had small quick eyes and a black needly beard and he seemed to despise me (too much as I thought) for a country bumpkin.

"Annie, have down the cut ham," I shouted, for my sister had come to the door by chance or because of the sound of a horse in the road, "and cut a few rashers of hung deer's meat. There is a gentleman come to sup, Annie. And draw some good ale."

"Bless me," said my new friend, "you are good folk, the right sort and no mistake."

"Then come," I said, "and my sister Annie will see to your comfort."

"In faith then, I will leave my horse in your hands and go in. Yet stay, I almost forgot my reason for coming. I may not rest nor eat until I have seen and touched John Ridd."

"Have no fear, good sir," I answered, "you have seen and touched John Ridd for I am he."

"Then in the name of the King, His Majesty, Charles the Second, receive *this*."

He touched me with the white thing which I had first seen him waving, and which I now saw to be sheepskin, such as they call parchment. It was tied across with cord, and fastened down in every corner with unsightly dabs of wax. By order of the King's Messenger, I broke the seals and there I saw my name in big letters. The parchment read as follows: To our good subject, John Ridd. Greeting. You are required, in the name of our Lord the King, to appear in person before the Right Worshipful the Justices of His Majesty's Bench at Westminster, and there to give evidence about certain matters by which the peace of our said lord the King and the well-being of this realm may be endangered." There were four seals after this and then a signature which I could not make out, only that it began with a J, and ended with some other writing, done almost in a circle. Underneath was added in a different handwriting. "Expenses will be paid. The matter is full urgent."

Seeing the expression on my face, the officer exclaimed, "My son, be not afraid. We are not going to skin you. I am only Jeremy Stickles, and nothing more than a poor servant of the Worshipful Court of King's Bench. And now, where is my supper?"

My mother and sisters were dumbfounded at the news that I must go to London by order of the King. Mother was convinced that her John was to be honoured, but I myself was deeply gone into the pit of sorrow. For what would Lorna think of me? The long month of waiting was over and there would be her lovely self, peeping softly down the glen and I would not be there. What an insult to her! Thinking about this, I could not sleep. I knew I must go and felt myself in a position of trust, for who could tell what the king might have to say to me about the Doones, and I felt that they were at the bottom of the strange order I had received.

Master Stickles and I had to leave the next day which was a Friday and Sunday was the very first day on which it would be honourable for me to enter Glen Doone. I would not be able to explain to Lorna and my only chance of seeing her before I went, lay in watching from the cliff and catching a glimpse of her or receiving a signal from her.

This, however, I did in vain until my eyes were weary. But though I lay hidden behind the trees upon the crest of the stony fall, and waited so quiet that the rabbits and squirrels played round me, and even the keen-eyed weasel took me for a trunk of wood, no sign of my beloved broke the loneliness of the vale.

Chapter XV

A journey to London seemed to us, in those bygone days, as hazardous and dark an adventure as could be forced on any man. Apart from the bad state of the roads there were highwaymen and foot-pads as well as straying soldiers and landlords of small inns who cheated their customers.

But nowadays it is very different. In this reign of good Queen Anne, we still have highwaymen but the roads are much improved and there are stage waggons, some of which can travel as much as forty miles on a summer day.

My heart was heavy but I kept up a cheerful manner when I parted from my mother and sisters although they were crying. As for Lorna, only the King's trust in me and the direct order could have persuaded me to leave without seeing her first and explaining, and I bitterly regretted that we had not arranged some system of signalling when I could not get to her. What would she think?

Jeremy Stickles, who was a kind man, did his best to

cheer me up with jokes and tales and descriptions of London life and, after a while, I began to long to see the things he was describing. He was much pleased with this and we became excellent friends.

We dined at Porlock with an old friend, having decided not to use our stores until we had to, and we lay that night at Dunster, in the house of a worthy tanner, first cousin to my mother, who received us very cordially, and undertook to return old Smiler to his stable at Plover's Barrows after one day's rest. From Dunster, we hired fresh horses to Bridgewater and from Bridgewater on to Bristowe, breaking the journey between the two. We were not troubled with highwaymen, for Tom Faggus had been to see Annie a few days before (something he did quite often), and when I let it be known that I was his cousin, there was not a house upon the road but was proud to entertain us.

Tom had been a very popular highwayman and many were sorry he had left the profession and become respectable.

It was a long and tiring journey of several days and the night was falling very thick by the time we were come to Tyburn. Here Jeremy Stickles decided that it would be wise to halt, because the way was unsafe by night across the fields to Charing Village. I was not sorry, for I wanted to see London by daylight.

And after all, it was not worth seeing, but a very hideous and dirty place, not at all like Exmoor. Some of the shops were very fine, and the signs above them finer still, so that I was never weary of standing still to look at them and annoyed the wayfarers who would bustle and scowl at me and draw their swords.

The only things that pleased me much were the river Thames, Westminster Abbey and Westminster Hall where there are brave things to be seen and braver still to think about, but whenever I wandered in the streets which were crowded and noisy I wished myself to be back among the sheep again.

I had been two months in London and had used up nearly all my mother's hard won money, when I was finally called to speak. Every day I had attended at Westminster Hall hoping to be summoned before the Law and becoming more and more worried about my family and the farm. Jeremy Stickles was on other business and I thought they had forgotten me. At last I was approached by a clerk who inquired my name and took me to a room which was lofty but dark, with wooden panels round it. At the further end were some raised seats, lined with velvet with a canopy over the middle one. This was the only one occupied.

The clerk bowed low, ushered me in and announced, "John Ridd, my Lord." I advanced as he had instructed me and stood, face to face, and alone with Judge Jeffreys, the Lord Chief Justice.

Chapter XVI

Judge Jeffreys bent his heavy brows upon me. He was infamous for his cruelty and I was frightened, but I stood straight in front of him and looked him in the eye. Then he spoke: "John Ridd, is there in your neighbourhood a certain band of robbers and outlaws whom all men fear to handle?"

"Yes, my lord. At least, I believe some of them are robbers and all of them are outlaws."

"And what is your high sheriff about, that he does not hang them all? Or send them up for me to hang without more ado?"

"I reckon that he is afraid, my lord; it is not safe to meddle with them. They are of good birth and reckless and hold a strong position in the county."

"Good birth! When has that ever saved a man who challenges the King and the Law? It is the surest way to the block to be the chip of an old one, and many such have I

70

sentenced to death. What is the name of this pestilent race, and how many of them are there?"

"They are the Doones of Bagworthy forest, may it please your worship. And we reckon there are about forty of them beside the women and children."

"Forty Doones, all forty thieves, and women and children! How long have they been there then?"

"They may have been there thirty years, my lord, and indeed, they may have been forty. It is longer back than I can remember."

"Ay, long before you were born, John. Good, you speak plainly. Woe betide a liar whenever I get hold of him. You need me in the West Country, by God, and you shall have me when the London traitors have all been hanged.

"Now, John Ridd," continued Judge Jeffreys, "have you ever seen a man whose name is Thomas Faggus?"

"Yes, sir, many and many a time. He is my own worthy cousin, and I fear he is over fond – " and here I stopped, having no right there to speak about my sister Annie.

"Tom Faggus is a good man," he said, and his great square face had a smile which showed me he had met my cousin.

"Now a few more things, John Ridd, and for the present I have done with you." My heart leaped up at the thought of getting away from London, and yet I could hardly trust to it.

"Are there any signs round your way of disloyalty to His Majesty, His most gracious Majesty?"

"No, my lord, no sign whatever. We pray for him in church and we talk about him afterwards, hoping our prayers may do him good. But after that we have nothing to say, not knowing much about him."

"That is as it should be, John. And the less you say the

better. But I have heard of traitorous talk and actions in Taunton, and even nearer to you in Dulverton, and even nearer still on Exmoor, but I see that you know nothing of them. Keep clear of all this, John. It will come to nothing, yet many shall swing high for it. Even I could not save you, if you were mixed up in this affair. Keep away from the Doones. I meant to use you as my spy, but I see you are too honest and simple. I will send another, but have nothing to do with the traitors and never let me find you being used by them or repeating my words to them."

Here the Lord Justice gave me such a glare, that I wished myself well rid of him, though thankful for his warnings, and seeing how he had left the mark of fear on me, he smiled and said, "Now get you gone, John Ridd. I shall remember you; and I think you will remember me."

I bowed low and left the Court and went in search of the attendant who had arranged for my expenses to be paid, but found there was nothing for me and I was told to go to the devil. In despair, I wandered into the street. I could walk home, but I must have food and shot and powder for my gun. I had just a crown piece left and I also needed shoes.

But I was saved by my good friend Jeremy Stickles who had newly come in search of me. I told him my story and he surprised me very much, by showing no surprise at all.

"It is the way of the world, John. They have got all they can from you, and why should they feed you further?"

That good friend gave me five pounds and said he would take his chance of getting it back from the rogue who served Judge Jeffreys. I said I would repay him, but he would take no written promise to pay from me and I could have kissed his hand for his goodness.

Chapter XVII

It was the beginning of wheat-harvest when I came to Dunster town, having walked all the way from London and being somewhat foot-sore. For though five pounds was enough to keep me in food and lodging upon the road, and leave me many a shilling to give to far poorer travellers, it would be nothing for horse-hire, as I knew too well by the prices Jeremy Stickles had paid upon our way to London. Now I never saw a prettier town than Dunster looked that evening, for, to tell the truth, I had almost lost all hope of reaching it that night, although I could see the castle far ahead. But being once there, my troubles were gone, for I stayed again with my mother's cousin, the worthy tanner, who was so indignant to see my weary and footsore condition, that he sent me off the next morning on the strongest horse he had. His gentle daughters came to wish me God speed and kissed their hands at the doorway. It made me proud and glad to think that, after seeing so much of the world, and having held my own with it, I was once more among my own people and found them kinder and more warm-hearted and better-looking too than almost anybody I had chanced upon in the mighty city of London.

Words cannot express my feelings as I drew near to our dear homestead. Old Smiler had told them that I was coming, for, having escaped from his halter-ring, he had come out to graze in the lane a bit, when what should he see but a strange horse coming with young master upon him? Then Smiler gave me a stare and a neigh with his tail quite stiff with amazement, and then he flung up his hind feet, and galloped straight home and set every dog wild with barking.

My mother and sisters held me tight and thanked God for my safe return but they were angry when I told them how I had been left without money for travelling home-ward and were inclined to blame the King. But I told them the King had nothing to do with it and I gave them their presents. Lorna's had been carried all the way next to my heart until I should see her again at last.

On the Sunday we all went to church and all the congregation stared at me, so that the parson was forced to remind them when to kneel down, and in the evening, after supper, we sat quietly round the fire while I told my dear ones all about London and my doings there which I was free to tell.

But on the Monday morning while my farm work lay before me, I was wondering how I could slip away to see Lorna and yet I knew that my first day's task on the farm would be strictly watched by every one, even by my gentle mother and Betty Muxworthy, to see what I had learned in London. But could I let another day pass, and Lorna think me faithless?

I felt much inclined to tell dear mother all about Lorna and how I loved her, yet had no hope of winning her. Often and often I had longed to do this, but the thought of my father's terrible death at the hands of the Doones prevented me. And it seemed to me foolish and mean to grieve mother when I did not know what Lorna felt about me. If once Lorna loved me, my mother should know it, and it would be the greatest happiness to me to have no concealment from her, though at first she was sure to grieve terribly. But I saw no more chance of Lorna loving me, than of the man in the moon coming down.

I decided to take a chance, worked with the men for a while until they were weary and unlikely to follow me, then strode away quickly resolved to face the worst of it and try to be home for supper.

I went first to the crest of the broken highland, from where I had agreed to watch for any sign or signal from Lorna. And sure enough at last I saw (when it was too late to see) that the white stone had been covered over with a cloth or mantel – the sign that something had happened to make Lorna want me. For a moment I stood amazed at my evil fortune that I had not been there when she needed me; then I set off to make the round of the outer cliffs as quickly as possible and climb up my usual way. It was not long, although to me it seemed an age, before I stood in the niche of rock at the head of the slippery watercourse, and gazed into the quiet glen where my foolish heart was dwelling and I was content that it should be so. There I waited.

At last a little figure came, looking very light and slender in the moving shadows. I rushed out at once, forgetting all danger, but Lorna looked frightened when I hoped for gladness.

I was taken aback and went slowly forward somewhat

distressed and said, "Mistress Lorna, I hoped that you needed me."

"Oh yes, but that was long ago, two months ago or more, sir." Saying this, she looked away as if it were all over. I felt overwhelmed with sorrow and I tried to turn away without another word, and go. But Lorna ran to me and held out both her hands. "Master Ridd," she whispered very softly, "I did not mean to hurt you." I took her hands but could not speak for fear of sobbing out loud.

"Come away from this bright place," said Lorna, trembling. "I am watched and spied on of late. Come into the shadows, John." We stole across the silent grass into her bower, now in its summer glory. Lorna slowly raised her eyes and looked at me shyly.

"Darling, do you love me?" was all that I could say to her.

"Yes, I like you very much," she answered, dropping her eyes.

"But do you love me, Lorna; do you love me more than all the world?"

"No, to be sure not. Now why should I?"

"In truth I know not why you should. Only I hoped that you did, Lorna. Either love me not at all, or, as I love you, for ever."

"John, I love you very much and I think of you every day, but why do you leave me for other people to do just as they like with me?"

"To do as they like! Oh, Lorna, not to make you marry Carver?"

"Not yet, for I am too young, but they wanted me to give my word and be formally betrothed to him in the presence of my grandfather, so that no other Doone could woo me. That was why I gave the sign that I wished to see you, John. I refused to do as they asked and now I am watched and spied upon and followed and half my little freedom seems to be taken from me. I could not be here speaking to you in my own little nook and refuge if it was not for the skill and courage of my dear little maid, Gwenny Carfax. She is now my greatest help and, through her alone, I hope to baffle all my enemies, since others have forsaken me."

Tears of sorrow and reproach were lurking in her soft, dark eyes, until in a few words I told her why I had gone away and of my bitter sorrow that I had been unable to tell her without putting her into more danger. When she heard all this, and saw the ring of pearls with a sapphire in the midst of them which I had bought in London, her gentle tears flowed fast, and she came and sat so close beside me that I trembled. I raised her left hand and tried to put the ring on her finger, but she drew back, touched it with her lips and told me to keep it until she had earned it. My hand stole round her waist, but she stood up quickly and said, laughing, "Now John, it is high time for you to go home to your mother. I love your mother very much from what you have told me about her, and I will not have her neglected."

"If you truly love my mother," said I very craftily, "the only way to show it is by truly loving me."

She laughed at me in the sweetest manner and I knew, as in a glory, that Lorna Doone had now begun, and would go on, to love me.

She asked me to stay away for two months because of our danger, but we arranged a system of signals and, as we parted, she said to me, "I have nothing now to fear, John. It is true that I am spied on and watched, but Gwenny is too clever for them. While I have my grandfather to prevent all violence, and little Gwenny to watch those who try to watch me, and you above all others, John, ready at a moment, if the worst comes to the worst, Lorna Doone will be safe. Therefore do not squeeze my hand, John; I am safe without it, and you do not know your strength."

Chapter XVIII

We had the best harvest for several years followed by much celebration, but I was uneasy. I remembered the warning of Judge Jeffreys and took note of some rumours that we heard on market days. There were tales of secret meetings and we knew for certain that at Taunton, Bridgewater and even Dulverton, there was a feeling growing against the King and his brother James and a wish to go back to the days of the Puritans. I had told the truth to Judge Jeffreys when I had assured his Lordship that to the best of my knowledge our people were loyal and there was no trouble brewing.

But now I was beginning to doubt whether I might not have been mistaken, especially when we heard, as we did, of arms being landed at Lynmouth in the dead of night, and of the tramp of men having reached someone's ears, from a hill where a famous echo was.

But how was it likely to be as to the Doones? Which side

would they probably take in the coming movement, if indeed there was to be one? So far as they had any religion at all, by birth they were Roman Catholics – this I knew from Lorna. On the other hand they were not likely to have any love for the son of the man who had banished them and confiscated their property. And it was not at all impossible that desperate men, such as they were, having nothing to lose but estates to recover and not being held much by the religion of their birth, should make common cause with a Protestant uprising, for the chances of revenge and a new ruler.

The harvest being done, and the thatching of the ricks made sure against southwestern tempests, and all the reapers being gone with good money and thankfulness, I began to burn in spirit for the sight of Lorna and on the last day of my eight weeks' exile I went in search of her, taking the pearl ring hopefully, and all the new-laid eggs I could find, and a dozen and a half of small trout from our brook. By this time I had told dear Annie my secret and she was the greatest comfort to me. We arranged that if, by any lucky chance, Lorna should invite me to sup with her in the bower, Annie would somehow account for my absence if I should be late.

But alas, I was utterly disappointed, for although I waited for hours, no Lorna ever appeared at all, not even the faintest sign of her. And something else happened which annoyed me more than it need have done, for so small a matter. And this was that my little offering of the trout, and the new-laid eggs, was carried off in the coolest manner by that vile Carver Doone. For, thinking to keep them fresh, I had laid them in a little bed of reeds by the side of the water, and placed some dog-leaves over them. I was watching from my hiding place beneath a willow tree, when I saw a great man coming slowly down the valley. He had a broad-brimmed hat and a leather jerkin and heavy jack boots to his middle thigh, and, what was worst of all for me, on his shoulder he bore a long rifle. Having nothing with me but my staff, I retired behind a rock, keeping the tree between us and peered out. As the great man drew nearer, I was able to distinguish his features and there was something in his face that turned me cold as though with a kind of horror. I felt certain that this was the man who had killed my father.

It was not an ugly face, but rather it seemed a handsome one, full of strength and resolution. From the short black hair above the broad forehead, to the long black beard descending beneath the short bold chin, there was nothing pleasant, no hint of humour and the steel-blue eyes were cold and aggressive. I knew that I was looking at my rival, Carver Doone.

As he passed along the margin of the stream, he noticed my little hoard covered up with dog-leaves. He saw that the leaves were upside down, and this of course drew his attention. I saw him stoop and uncover the fish and eggs and thought that they had given me away. But, to my surprise, he seemed amused, and his harsh short laughter came to me without echo.

"Aha! Now which of them is paying court to my Lorna? I shall roast him tonight when I find out, and that I surely will."

With this, he calmly packed up my fish, and all the best of dear Annie's eggs, and went off chuckling.

I hastened home very sadly, and the wind of early autumn moaned across the moorland. All the beauty of harvest time was gone and the early fall of dusk was like a weight upon me. Nevertheless, I went every evening for a fortnight, hoping every time to see my love. And meanwhile what puzzled me most was that the signals appeared in order as we had arranged, so that I thought Lorna could not be a prisoner. I decided on my next visit to come at a different time.

It was early one October morning that I again sought Lorna and this time I saw her coming down the valley, purer than the morning dew, than the sun more bright and clear.

As she drew nearer, I came from my hiding place, the bloom on her cheeks was deepened, and the radiance of her eyes, and she came to meet me gladly.

"At last you have come, John. I could not make you understand by the signs that, in the evening, they are keeping me prisoner, but in the morning I am free. Come into my little house; you are not safe here."

Meanwhile I could not answer, being overcome with joy, but followed to her little grotto where I had been twice before. I knew that the crowning moment of my life was coming – that Lorna would own her love for me. She pretended for a while not to understand the meaning of my gaze, but tried to speak of other things and not meeting my eyes.

"This is not what I came to talk about," I whispered very softly; "you know what I have come to ask."

"If you have come on purpose to ask anything, why do you delay so?" She turned away very bravely, but I saw that her lips were trembling.

"Lorna, I have loved you long and long," I said, being reckless now. "I love you more than tongue can tell. I must have all your heart as you have mine. Tell me that I have it."

"Darling, you have won it all. I shall never be my own again. I am yours, my own one for ever and ever." I kissed her hand then and slipped my little ring upon the wedding finger; and this time Lorna kept it, and looked with fondness on its beauty, and clung to me with a flood of tears.

"Darling," said I, drawing her closer to me, "you shall weep no more, but live in peace and happiness with me to guard and cherish you and none shall dare to frighten you or make you sad again."

"It is a dream," she murmured to herself. "Something in my heart tells me it can be so never, never."

Chapter XIX

There was, however, no possibility of depressing me at such a time. To be loved by Lorna, the fairest creature on God's earth, the lady of high birth and mind, and that I a mere yeoman farmer had won that loving heart to be my own for ever, was a thought that no fears could overcome and no chance could steal from me.

She begged me now with a kiss to hurry home and this I did in great happiness, yet with some misgivings, for Lorna had made me promise now to tell my mother everything. I had always meant to do this if I was successful in winning Lorna, but, because a Doone had killed my father, I knew it would not be easy. In spite of that, knowing my mother's tenderness and deep affection for me, I was sure that once she saw Lorna, she would so love and glory in her that she would feel quite differently about our love and would praise and thank me, undeserving though I was.

Unfortunately for my plans, who should be sitting

down at breakfast with my mother and the rest but Squire Faggus, as everybody now began to call him? I noticed something odd about him, something uncomfortable in his manner, and a lack of that ease and humour which he usually had about him. He took his breakfast as it came, without a single joke about it, or liking this or that, but with sly soft looks at Annie, who seemed unable to sit quiet, or to look anyone in the face. I feared in my heart what was coming and felt truly sorry for poor mother.

After breakfast it became my duty to see to the ploughing of some barley stubble ready for the sowing of french grass, and I asked Tom Faggus to come with me; but he refused and I knew the reason. I resolved to give him a clear field though I was not pleased that a man of his reputation should marry into our family which had always been counted so honest. I therefore carried my dinner upon my back, and spent the whole day with the furrows.

When I returned, Squire Faggus had gone, but Lizzie came running to meet me at the bottom of the wood-rick and cried, "Oh John, there is such a to-do. Mother is in such a state of mind, and Annie crying her eyes out. What do you think? You would never guess, though I have suspected it ever so long."

"No need for me to guess," I replied, "I knew all about it long ago. You have not been crying much, I see. I should like you better if you had."

"Why should I cry? I like Tom Faggus. He is the only one I ever see with the spirit of a man."

This was, of course, a cut at me, but I ignored it and we entered the house together. Mother sent at once for me, while I was trying to console my darling sister Annie.

"Oh John! Speak one good word for me," she cried with both hands laid in mine, and her tearful eyes looking up at me.

"Not one, my pet, but a hundred," I answered, putting

my arm round her. "Have no fear, Annie. I am going to make your case so bright by comparison with mine, that mother will send for you in five minutes and call you her best of daughters, and praise cousin Tom to the skies, and send a man on horseback after him, and then you will have a harder task to speak for me, my dear."

"Oh John, dear John, you won't tell her about Lorna – oh not today, dear."

"Yes, today, and at once, Annie. I want to have it over, and be done with it."

"But think of her, dear. I am sure she could not bear it after the shock of my news today."

"She will bear it all the better," said I; "the one will drive the other out. I know exactly what mother is. She will be desperately savage first with you, and then with me, and then for a very little while both of us together, but before very long (particularly if we both keep out of the way) she will begin to think that after all she has been a little too hasty, and then she will remember how good we have always been to her, and how like our father. Upon that, she will think of her own love-time, and sigh a good bit, and cry a little, and then smile, and send for both of us and beg our pardon, and call us her two darlings."

"Now John, how on earth can you know all that?" exclaimed my sister, wiping her eyes and gazing at me with a soft bright smile. "Who on earth can have told you that, John?"

"Never you mind," I replied, with a nod of some conceit, I fear. "I must be a fool if I did not know what mother is by this time."

Things turned out exactly as I had said they would and, by the afternoon, when the sun began to go down upon us, our mother sat on the garden bench with her head on my waistcoat and her right arm round our Annie's waist, and scarcely knowing which of us she ought to make the most of, or which deserved most pity. Not that she had forgiven yet the rivals to her love – Tom Faggus, I mean, and Lorna – but that she was beginning to think a little better of them now, and a vast deal better of her own children. Surely a better mother never lived and I cannot add another word to that. Lizzie behaved very well for her and indeed was much to be pitied, for although she had beautiful eyes, hands and feet and a neck as white as snow, she was awkward and had not our abounding health and this sometimes made her irritable and critical of other people's happiness.

Mother finally gave her blessing to Annie and Tom just as I said she would, but it was more difficult for Lorna and me. It was a comfort that I had told mother, but although she longed to see Lorna, she made me promise not to risk my life by needless visits and this made matters easier. It was left to my own good sense to decide when to go. Fortunately I had not told her of my narrow escape from Carver Doone.

I went to see Lorna soon after I had talked with my mother to tell her all about it. My beauty gave me one sweet kiss with all her heart and I begged for one more to take to our mother and, before leaving, I obtained it. I told her how my mother and Annie, as well as I, longed to have her at Plover's Barrows, but she answered with a bright blush, that while her grandfather was living, she would never leave him, and that even if she were free, certain ruin would be brought on any family receiving her which was within reach of the Doones.

I could not deny this, and seeing me cast down, she told me bravely that we must hope for better times and, as I had bound her, so she bound me with an ancient gold ring which she had had on her necklace for as long as she could remember. I recognized it as a thumb ring, having dug up one or two whilst ploughing, and I told her it should go to the grave with me. And so it shall, unless there are villains who would rob the dead. But before I got used to wearing it, and my family had stopped admiring it, we all had something else to think of, not so pleasant, and more puzzling than a ring.

Chapter XX

Now November was upon us. We had kept All Saints' Day and soon afterwards there were Guy Fawkes bonfires and then, while we were sowing wheat, another visitor arrived.

This was Master Jeremy Stickles, who had been a good friend to me in London and had earned my mother's gratitude, so far as he ever chose to have it. And he seemed inclined to have it all, for he made our farmhouse his headquarters, and kept us quite at his beck and call, going out at any time of the evening, and coming back at any time of the morning, and always expecting us to be ready, whether with horse, or man, or maidens, or fire, or provisions. We knew that he was employed somehow upon the service of the King, and had at different places certain troopers and orderlies quite at his disposal. Also we knew that he never went out, nor even slept in his bedroom, without heavy firearms well loaded, and a sharp sword to hand and that he had a special commission from the King whereby all persons from highest to lowest rank had to assist him or answer to it at their peril.

One day, seeing that I was to be trusted, he asked me if I had heard much in London about the Duke of Monmouth.

"Not so very much," I answered, "not half so much as in Devonshire where I heard he was a hearty man, and a very handsome one, and now was banished by the government, and most people wished he was coming back. They like him better than the Duke of York."

"Things are changed since you were in town. There is unrest everywhere, and it must grow to an outbreak. The King has many troops in London and means to bring over more from Tangier in North Africa, but he cannot command these country places and there are those who do not want King Charles to be succeeded as King by his brother James."

"I am loyal to the King," I said, "but as to who comes after, God knows, I have no politics."

"Stick to that, my lad," answered Master Stickles. "I think I am safe to tell you that I am here to watch the gathering of a secret plot, not so much against the King as against the Duke of York as his successor." I told him that I understood, but I hoped in my heart that I should not be drawn in on either side and I kept his confidence.

But now my own affairs were thrown into such disorder that I could think of nothing else, and had the greatest difficulty in hiding my uneasiness. For suddenly, without any warning, or any message, all my Lorna's signals ceased. Three times I went, and waited long at the bottom of the valley, where now the stream was brown and angry with the rains of autumn, and the weeping trees hung leafless. But though I waited at every hour of day and far into the night, no light footstep came to meet me, no sweet voice was in the air, and all was lonely, drear and drenched with sodden desolation. It seemed as if my love was dead and the winds were at her funeral.

Once I went far up the valley where I had never been before. Following up the river channel in the shelter of the evening fog, I reached a corner within a stone's throw of the last outlying cottage. This was a gloomy, low, square house, without any light in the windows, roughly built of wood and stone, as I saw when I drew nearer. I thought, from something that Lorna had said that this must be Carver's dwelling. I was led by curiosity, and perhaps by jealousy, to have a closer look at it. Therefore, I crept up the stream, too worried about Lorna to be frightened. And in truth there was not too much to fear, the sky being now too dark for even a shooter of wild fowl to take good aim. And nothing else but guns could hurt me because of my strength and my skill with my single-stick.

Nevertheless I went carefully being among enemies. The back of Carver's house was right by the waves of the rushing stream, and seeing a loophole meant for a gun, I looked, but all was quiet. So far as I could judge by listening, there was no one now inside, and my heart for a moment leaped with joy, for I had feared to find Lorna there. Then I made a careful survey of the building, its windows and doors as if I were a robber planning to break in. It was a good thing for me later on that I had done this.

I would have gone further up the village, but a bar of red light across the river, some forty yards on above me and crossing from the opposite side like a chain, prevented me. In that second house there was a gathering of loud and merry Doones, making as much noise as if they had the law on their side.

I started cautiously for home, resolving as I went that I would penetrate Glen Doone from the upper end and find out what had happened to my Lorna, and my last thought as I fell asleep that night was that the danger was nothing compared with losing my darling.

Chapter XXI

The enterprise I had now decided upon was far more dangerous than anything I had attempted before and I therefore went to Porlock to see Mr Tape, the lawyer, and made my will. The thought of death did not deter me, for it was a choice between two evils, of which by far the greater one was, of course, to lose Lorna.

The journey was a great deal longer to skirt the Southern hills and enter by the Doone-gate, than to cross the lower land and steal in by the waterslide. I started early in the evening so as not to hurry or waste any strength upon the way. And thus I came to the robbers' highway walking cautiously, scanning the skyline of every hill, and searching the folds of every valley for any moving figure.

Although it was now well on towards dark, I could see the robbers' road before me in a trough of the winding hills where a brook ran down beside it and the banks were roofed with furze. I could see no one, but waited until twilight melted into night and then I crept down a rocky path and stood upon the Doone track.

As the road approached the entrance, it became more straight and strong, like a channel cut from rock. Not a tree or bush was left to shelter a man from bullets. All was stern and stiff and rugged and a sense of being boxed in made me long to be out again.

And here I was unlucky for, as I reached the entrance, the moon came out, topping the eastward edge of rock, and filling all the open spaces with its wavering light. I shrank back into the shadowy quarter on the right side of the road and studied the triple entrance on which the moonlight fell askew.

Across the three rough archways hung a felled oak, black and thick and threatening. This, I had heard, could be let fall in a moment, so as to crush a score of men, and bar the approach of horses. Behind this tree, the rocky mouth was spanned, as by a gallery, with brushwood and piled timber, all upon a ledge of stone, where thirty men might lurk unseen and fire at any invader. From that rampart it would be impossible to dislodge them, because the rock fell sheer below them twenty feet or more, while overhead it towered three hundred, and jutted over in such a way that nothing could be thrown down upon them, even if a man could climb that high. Three rocky chambers led to this fortress-like place, all being pretty much alike and I had heard that, in times of danger, they changed the entrance every day and, by means of sliding doors, led intruders down the other paths to deep chasms and dark abysses.

Now I could see those three rough arches, jagged, black, and I knew that only one of them could lead me to the Doone valley. The river was no help, for it dived underground with a sullen roar, where it met the cross-bar of the mountain. I hesitated, having no means of judging which arch to choose and knowing that the other two would lead to almost certain death. Then I decided that in times of peace, the middle was the likeliest so, keeping up my courage, I plunged into the middle way, holding a long ash staff before me, shodden at the end with iron. I went on in the darkness for quite a way until suddenly I saw a light and peering round a corner, saw two sentries. I drew back and laid one cheek to the rock face keeping my outer eye around the jutting out bit and wondered how long I would have to wait before I could get past.

The two villains were drinking and gambling and becoming quarrelsome. The money which changed hands from time to time lay before them. Presently, as I made up my mind to steal along towards them (for the cavern was pretty wide just there), the younger and taller man reached forth his hand and seized a pile of coins claiming that he had won the last throw. Upon this, the other jerked his arm, vowing that he had no right to it and the first man flung at his face the contents of the glass he was sipping, but he missed him and hit the candle inside their lantern and it fluttered and went out. At this, one swore, and the other laughed, and before they had settled what to do, I was past them and round the corner.

I went on as steadily as I could in the darkness until I began to hear footsteps behind me and getting nearer. It was light enough now for me to see that it was the younger of the gamblers lurching along drunkenly. I flattened myself against the wall, hoping that he would not see me and that if I followed him, he would eventually lead me to the Doone village. I was lucky, for he stumbled on past me and led me finally to the top of the meadow land, where the stream from underground broke forth, seething quietly with a little hiss of bubbles. From here I could see the robbers' township, spread with bushes here and there and well lit by the moon.

I knew that the Captain's house was first, both from what Lorna had said of it and from my mother's description at the time they killed my father and I saw the robber pause for a moment and look up at one of the windows. Then he went on down the village and I followed him carefully, keeping as much as possible in the shadowy places and watching the windows of every house, to see if any light were burning. As I passed Sir Ensor's house, my heart leaped up, for I spied a window, higher than the rest above the ground, and with a faint light moving. This could hardly fail to be Lorna's room for here the robber had looked up and I cursed him for his impudence but at least if she was there it meant that she was with her grandfather and not at Carver's accursed dwelling.

Relieved at this, I hurried after the robber and then, while I watched from behind a tree, the door of the furthest house was opened, and sure enough it was Carver who stood there, bare-headed and half undressed. I could see his great black hairy chest by the light of the lamp he bore.

"What do you want, Charlie?" he said in a deep, gruff voice. "You are supposed to be standing sentry tonight."

"I'll not keep you, Master Carver. All I want is a light for my lantern and a glass of spirits if you have it."

"You have had enough already," grumbled Carver as he kindled the lantern. "Be off! My patience is done with."

Then he slammed the door in the young man's face and Charlie went back on guard, muttering as he unknowingly passed me, "Bad look-out for all of us, when that surly old beast is Captain. I'd get away from here if it wasn't for the girls."

My heart was in my mouth, when I stood in the shadow by Lorna's window and whispered her name as loudly as I dared. Lorna came to the window at once and drew back the curtain timidly. Then she opened it but, not having recognized my voice, was starting to shut it again when I held it back and showed myself.

"John!" she cried, yet with sense enough not to speak aloud, "oh, you must be mad, John."

"As mad as a March hare," said I, "without any news of my darling. You knew I would come. Of course you did."

"Well I hoped perhaps – . Do you see they have put iron bars across?"

"What is the meaning of it," I whispered, just managing to get hold of her hand, "why are you imprisoned here? Why have I had no signal? Has your grandfather turned against you and are you in any danger?"

"My poor grandfather is very ill and I fear he will not live long. The Counsellor and his son Carver are now the masters of the valley and I dare not come out for fear of what they might do to me. Little Gwenny is not allowed to leave the valley now, so I was not able to send you a message. I have been so wretched, dear. I was afraid you might think me false to you."

Before I could reply, she put up a finger and whispered, "I hear the old nurse moving. Grandfather is sure to send for me. Keep back from the window."

However, it was only Gwenny Carfax, Lorna's little handmaid. My darling brought her to the window and presented her to me, almost laughing through her grief. "Gwenny, this is my John. It is rather dark, but you can see him. I wish you to know him again, Gwenny."

"Whoy!" cried Gwenny with great amazement, standing on tiptoe to look out, and staring as if she were weighing me. "He be bigger nor any Doone!"

"Well, Gwenny, shall you know me again?"

"I shall knoo thee again, young man, no fear of that," she answered, nodding her head. "Now, missis, go on courtin' and I'll go aside and keep watch."

"I love you far too much for you to stay, John," said Lorna. "Dear, darling John, if you love me, go."

"How can I go without settling anything?" I asked very sensibly. "How shall I know of your danger now? You are so quick; think of something."

"I have been thinking," Lorna answered rapidly in her sweet, clear voice. "You see that tree with the seven rooks' nests, bright against the cliffs there? Can you count them from above, do you think? From a safe place, of course."

"I am sure I can. It will not take me long to find such a place."

"Gwenny can climb like any cat. She has been up there in the summer, watching the young birds, day by day, and daring the boys to touch them. There are neither birds, nor eggs there now, of course, and nothing happening there. If you see but six rooks' nests, I am in peril and want you. If you see but five, I have been carried off by Carver."

"Good God!" said I at the mere idea, in a tone which frightened Lorna.

"Do not fear, John," she whispered sadly, "he may seize me, but he shall never hold me. Dead or alive, you will know that I have been true to you." Her face was full of pride and I could only answer, "God bless you, my darling." She said the same to me in a very low, sad voice and then I stole away, knowing enough of the village now to find her in case of necessity.

A weight of care was off my mind, though I was still deeply troubled. One thing was quite certain – if Lorna could not have John Ridd, no one else should have her.

Chapter XXII

And now a thing came to pass which tested my love pretty sharply because I would far rather have faced Carver Doone and his father, than have met, in cold blood, Sir Ensor Doone, the founder of all the colony and dreaded by even the fiercest of the Doones.

But I was forced to do it, and it happened like this: When I went up one morning to look for my seven rooks' nests, I could see only six. I knew that this meant my love was in danger. For me to enter the valley now in broad daylight could have brought only harm to Lorna and certain death for myself, so I waited until darkness was coming on and then set off taking my dog Watch with me. There was frost in the air and later in the week it led to great difficulties on the farm and for Lorna and me. I was among trees and preparing to go up into the hills, when suddenly Watch gave a long, low growl. I kept as quiet as possible and ordered the dog to be silent, and presently saw a short figure approaching from a thickly-wooded hollow on the left. It proved to my great delight to be the little maid Gwenny Carfax. She started a moment at seeing me, but more with surprise than fear and then she laid both her hands upon mine, as if she had known me for twenty years.

"Young man," she said, "you must come with me. Old man be dying and he can't die, or he won't, without seeing thee."

"Seeing me!" I cried, "what can Sir Ensor Doone want with seeing me? Has Mistress Lorna told him about us?"

"All about thee and thy doings, when she knowed old man was so near his end and he has sent for thee."

I was shaken but knew that I must either go straight to the presence of Sir Ensor Doone, or give up Lorna once for all and rightly be despised by her. For the first time in my life, I thought that she had not acted fairly. Why not leave the old man in peace, without worrying him about my affairs? But presently I saw that she was right. She could not receive the old man's dying blessing while she deceived him about herself and the life she had undertaken. Therefore, not at all sure of myself, but with no ill thought of my darling, I sent Watch home, and followed Gwenny who led me along very rapidly, down the hollow from which she had first appeared. Here at the bottom, she entered a thicket of grey ash and black holly and in a dark and lonely corner, she came to a narrow door, very brown and solid, looking like a trunk of wood at a little distance. This she opened without a key by stooping down and pressing it at the bottom and then she ran in very nimbly, but I was forced to be bent in two and the passage was close and difficult and as dark as pitch, but not very long and that was a comfort. We came out soon at the other end and found ourselves at the top of Doone valley.

As we crossed towards the Captain's house, we met a couple of great Doones lounging by the waterside. Gwenny said something to them and, although they stared very hard at me, they let me pass without hindrance. It is not too much to say that, when the little maid opened Sir Ensor's door, my heart thumped, quite as much with terror as with the hope of seeing Lorna. But in a moment my fear was gone, for Lorna was trembling in my arms. She feared that I would be cross with her for telling her grandfather about us and for dragging me into his presence, but I told her what was almost true that as long as I had her love, I cared not a fig for Sir Ensor Doone.

Lorna led me into a cold, dark room, rough and very gloomy, although with two candles burning. I took little heed of the things in it, though I noticed that the window was open.

The old man, very stern and handsome, with death upon his countenance, was not lying on his bed, but sitting upright on his chair with a loose red cloak thrown over him. Upon this his white hair fell and his pale fingers lay without life or movement. And in his great black eyes fixed upon me solemnly all the life of his soul was burning. I bowed and Lorna left the room, leaving us alone.

"Ah," said the old man, "are you that great John Ridd?"

"John Ridd is my name, your honour," I answered, "and I hope your worship is better."

"John Ridd, have you sense enough to know what you have been doing?"

"Yes, I know right well," I answered, "that I have set my eyes far above my rank."

"Do you not know that Lorna Doone is born of one of the oldest families remaining in North Europe?"

"I did not know that, your worship, yet I knew of her high descent from the Doones of Bagworthy."

"And you know of your own low descent from the Ridds of Oare?"

"Sir," I answered, "the Ridds of Oare have been honest men twice as long as the Doones have been rogues."

"I would not answer for that, John," Sir Ensor replied, very quietly, though I expected fury, "but I forbid you ever to see that foolish child again. You will pledge your word in Lorna's presence, never to see or to speak to her again, never even to think of her. Now call her, for I am weary." He kept his great eyes fixed upon me with their icy fire and then he raised one hand and pointed to the door. I made a low bow and went straightway to find Lorna.

I found my love crying softly at a little window and listening to the river's grief. I put my left arm round her waist, and she put her right hand in mine and we walked bravely into the old man's presence.

Old Sir Ensor looked much astonished. For forty years he had been obeyed and feared by all around him and he knew that I had feared him vastly before I began to love Lorna.

"You two fools!" he said at last with a depth of contempt which no words can describe. "You two fools!"

"May it please your worship," I answered softly, "maybe we are not such fools as we look. But even if we are, we are well content, as long as we may be two fools together."

"Why, John," said Sir Ensor, almost smiling, "you are not altogether the country yokel I took you for."

"Oh no, grandfather, dear grandfather," cried Lorna, "nobody knows what John Ridd is because he is so modest. I mean, nobody except me, dear." And here she turned to me, and rose upon tiptoe and kissed me.

There was a long silence; the old man leaned back in his chair and sighed wearily. Was he thinking of his own lost youth?

"Fools you are," he said, "be fools for ever. It is the best I can wish you; boy and girl, be boy and girl, until you have grandchildren."

Partly in bitterness he spoke, and partly in pure weariness, and then he turned so as not to see us, and his white hair fell like a shroud around him.

Chapter XXIII

Sir Ensor Doone died the next day without giving formal consent to our marriage, although he had spoken of our future grandchildren. We like to think that had he lived a little longer, he might have bestowed his blessing on us. But he did give Lorna back her glass necklace which he had kept for safety and from which my ring had come.

There was great sorrow among the Doones and their women when he died, and we were sad too because at least he was a brave and courteous gentleman. The people around Exmoor regretted his death not only from fear that a wicked man might succeed him (as appeared only too probable), but from true admiration of his strong will and sympathy with his misfortunes. Carver and Counsellor never came near him before he died. They were too busy plotting for Carver to take Sir Ensor's place as head of the Doones.

Before Sir Ensor Doone was buried, the greatest frost of

the century had set in. I was allowed by the Doones to attend the funeral with Lorna and our breath was almost freezing on the air.

When it was all over, I strode across the moors very sadly, trying to keep the cold away by moving quickly. All the birds were flying westward and now I began to think about our farm animals. The next day we awoke to heavy snow. It was so thick that the men and I could barely open our doors as we hastened to save the sheep. With spades and shovels and pitchforks we dug them out and the poor things knew that it was high time. If it hadn't been for Watch, I don't think we should have found many of them. While Watch guarded the flock, we carried sixty-six in pairs, one under each arm and put them in the sheep-fold and the work grew harder each time as the drifts of snow were deepening. We lost many of the sheep who were on the mountain and many of our cattle too for the sheer impossibility of finding them. As for the house and farm, we were completely snowed up except where we had dug ourselves out by constant shovellings.

This terrible weather kept Tom Faggus from visiting Annie and me from going to Lorna. I was anxious about her, especially as she now had no protection, and the weather got worse as the days went on.

Then Lizzie, who is clever and reads a good deal, told me how the eskimos live and suggested I should make some snowshoes.

Following her description, I set to at once and, being used to thatching work, and the making of traps and so on, before very long I had built myself a pair of strong and light snowshoes, framed with ash and ribbed with willow, with half-tanned calf-skin stretched across, and an inner sole to support my feet. At first I could not walk at all and floundered about in the snowdrifts much to the

105

amuscment of my sisters, but things gradually improved until, with my mother's anxious blessing, I felt ready to set off for Glen Doone.

Chapter XXIV

When I started on my road across the hills and valleys, the utmost I could hope to do was to gain the crest of the hills, and look into the Doone Glen. From there I might at least see whether Lorna was still safe, by the six nests still remaining, and the view of the Captain's house.

Through the sparkling breadth of white which dazzled my eyes, and past the humps of trees laden with snow and bowing their backs like a woodman, I managed to get along, half sliding and half walking. Although there had been such a violent frost every night upon the snow, the snow itself, having never thawed even for an hour, had never coated over and was as soft and light as if it had fallen yesterday.

At last I got to my spy-hill and it was hard to find, for all the beautiful Glen Doone was covered half up the sides and at either end with snow. Not a patch of grass was there, not a black branch of a tree. All was white and the little river flowed beneath an arch of snow, if it managed to flow at all.

Now this was a great surprise to me, not only because I believed Glen Doone to be a place outside all frost, but also because it seemed to me that it was quite impossible to be cold near Lorna. It struck me all at once that Lorna and Gwenny might be in grave difficulties, so seeing no Doones were about, I resolved to slide the cliffs and bravely go to Lorna.

The snow was coming on again; I set my back and elbows against a snowdrift hanging far down the cliff, and saying some of the Lord's Prayer, threw myself on Providence. Before there was time to think or dream, I landed very beautifully upon a ridge of snow piled up in a quiet corner. My snowshoes stopped me from going far into it, and I stood up in good spirits and made off boldly across the valley (where the snow was furrowed hard) being now afraid of nobody.

When I came to the Captain's house, I went quietly to the door and knocked in a hesitating manner, not being sure if I might be facing a gun. I heard a pattering of feet and a whispering going on, and then a shrill voice through the keyhole asking, "Who's there?"

"Only me, John Ridd," I answered; upon which I heard a little laughter, and a little sobbing, or something that was like it, and then the door was opened about a couple of inches, but with the bar behind it still up, and then the little voice went on, "Put thy finger in young man with the old ring on it. But mind, if it be the wrong ring, thou shall never get it back again."

Laughing at Gwenny's mighty threat, I showed my finger through the opening. She let me in and barred the door again like lightning.

"What is the meaning of all this, Gwenny?" I asked as I

slipped about on the floor, for I could not stand there firmly with my great snowshoes on.

"Us be shut in here and starving," said the Cornish girl, "and we durstn't let anybody in upon us. My mistress is very poorly." She led me to another room where I found my darling half fainting in a chair and as white as the snow around us. I sat beside her and fanned her and rubbed her hand and presently she opened her eyes and whispered, "I never expected to see you again. I had made up my mind to die, John, and to die without your knowing it."

"You are hungry dear," I said, "and so is poor Gwenny."

I produced some nice food, carefully prepared by Annie, but Lorna would not taste a morsel until she had thanked God for it, and given me the kindest kiss and put a piece of mince pie in Gwenny's mouth.

When they had satisfied the first pangs of hunger, I asked them to tell me the meaning of their sad state.

"The meaning is sad enough," said Lorna, "and I see no way out of it. We are both to be starved until I let them do what they like with me."

"That is to say, until you choose to marry Carver Doone, and be slowly killed by him."

"Slowly! No John, quickly. I hate him with such bitterness, that less than a week would kill me."

"Not a doubt of that," said Gwenny. "She hates him, but not half so much as I do."

I told them both that this state of things could be endured no longer, and on this point they both agreed with me, but we were at a loss to know what to do, for even if Lorna could make up her mind to come away with me and live at Plover's Barrows farm under my good mother's care as I had urged so often, behold the snow was all around us, heaped as high as mountains and really impossible for maidens to cross.

109

Then I spoke with a strange tingle in my heart, knowing that this undertaking was a serious one for all, and might cause the Doones to burn our farm down.

"Lorna, will you come with me?"

"To be sure I will, dear," said my beauty with a smile, "I must starve or go with you, John."

"Gwenny, have you courage for it? Will you come with your young mistress?"

"Will I stay behind?" cried Gwenny in a voice that settled it.

And so we began to arrange about it, and I was much excited. It was useless now to leave it longer. If it was to be done at all, it must be done quickly. It was the Counsellor who had ordered, after all other schemes had failed, that his niece should have no food until she would obey him. He had strictly watched the house, taking turns with Carver to make sure no one came near it, but this evening, because of the weather, they thought it needless to remain on guard and it would have been impossible because they were holding a festival in honour of the new Captain of the Doone outlaws.

While we were discussing what to do, I saw far down the bed of the stream a little form of fire rising, red and dark and flickering. Presently it caught on something, and went upwards boldly, and then it split into many forks, and then it fell and rose again.

"They are firing their beacon," said Lorna, "in honour of Carver Doone."

At first I thought that this light would make our escape more difficult and then I realized that, during the festival, all the Doones would be drunk in about three hours' time and getting more and more in drink as the night went on. As for the fire, it would go down in about three hours or more and then there would only be helpful shadows. But

110

then the men would be more than ever dangerous to Lorna and Gwenny, so little time must be lost.

I turned at once to Lorna and told her what must be done.

"Sweetest, in two hours' time, I shall again be with you. Keep the bar across the door and have Gwenny ready to answer any one. You are safe while they are feasting and drinking healths. Before they have finished that, I shall be back. Bring any things you both need in one small bag. I shall knock loud, and then wait a little, and then knock twice very softly. Be ready and expect a joyful welcome in your new home."

Chapter XXV

I was at my wit's end how to get Lorna and Gwenny out, the passage by the Doone-gate being long and dark and difficult and leading to such a weary track among the snowy moors and hills. The other ways were hazardous and impossible for two half-starved maidens to manage.

But now, being homeward bound by the shortest possible track for me, I slipped along between the bonfire and the boundary cliffs, where I found a caved way of snow behind a sort of avalanche where I was unobserved. I was about to climb the cliff to go across the mountains when it struck me that I would just have a look at my first and painful entrance, the waterslide, and see what it was like under snow. But to my very great surprise there was scarcely any snow there at all, though plenty curling high overhead from the cliff like bolsters over it and the waterslide itself was less a slide than a path of ice. I realized it would be an easy track for my sledge with Lorna and

Gwenny sitting in it. The danger, though, would be the overhead snow and the black whirlpool at the bottom, the middle of which was still unfrozen, and looked more horrible than ever.

I hastened home at my utmost speed and asked my mother and Annie to make all preparations and I said something nice to Eliza in case she should be disagreeable to my love. Dear mother smiled at my excitement, though her own was not much less I'm sure and with it was great anxiety.

Next I took out our new light pony sledge, but I dared not take the pony as his hoofs would have gone through the snow, so I made a harness with some rope and decided to pull the sledge myself. I put in some provisions and two or three fur coats and one sealskin most kindly lent by mother.

Not daring to risk the sledge by any fall from the valley-cliffs, I dragged it very carefully up the steep incline of ice, through the narrow opening in the rock and right to the place where I had first seen my Lorna in the fishing days of boyhood. I moored the sledge and set off up the valley, skirting along one side of it.

The bonfire was still burning and a few children were playing round it watched by their mothers. The men were nowhere to be seen and I guessed they were probably drinking in some of the houses. I came without difficulty or interference to the door of Lorna's house and made the signal.

They came at once. I caught up my own darling and telling Gwenny to follow me, or else I would come back for her if she could not walk in the snow, I ran the whole distance to my sledge, not caring if anyone saw us or not. Then by the time I had put in Lorna, beautiful and smiling, with the sealskin over her, sturdy Gwenny came along, having trudged in the track of my snowshoes, although she had two bags on her back. I put her in beside her mistress and then, with one look back at the glen, which for so long had been the home of my heart, I hung on behind the sledge and launched it down the steep and dangerous way.

Though the cliffs were black above us, and the road unseen in front and a great white grave of snow might at a single word come down, Lorna was calm and happy because she was with me. Gwenny was frightened but I did my best to quieten her as, with a strong staff to steady us from rock to rock, I threw my weight backward to slow down the sledge and brought my love safely out by the same route which had first brought me to her.

Unpursued, yet looking back as if someone must be after us, we skirted round the black whirling pool and gained the meadows beyond it. Here there was hard collar work, the track being all uphill and rough, and Gwenny wanted to jump out, to lighten the sledge and push behind. But I would not hear of it because it was now so deadly cold and her nose was already touched with frost because she would not keep it quiet and snug beneath the sealskin. I stole a glance at Lorna beneath the folds of her cloak. She was pale and asleep, and I pulled the sledge on as hard as I could.

And so, in about an hour's time, we came to the old courtyard and all the dogs greeted us with joy. My heart was quivering, and my cheeks were as hot as the Doone's bonfire, with wondering both what Lorna would think of our farmyard, and what my mother would think of her.

We came to the house and all the people were at the open door. First, of course, Betty Muxworthy, teaching me how to draw up the sledge as if she had been born in it, and flourishing with a great broom, wherever a speck of

114

snow lay. Then dear Annie, and behind her mother, looking shy for her, and in the distance Lizzie stood, not willing to give encouragement, but unable to keep out of it. Gwenny had jumped out to help, but Lorna lay still asleep.

Dear mother's hands were quick and trembling, as she opened the folds of the cloak and saw my Lorna sleeping. She bent and kissed her forehead, and only said, "God bless her, John," as the tears poured from her eyes.

They carried her into the house, Betty chattering all the while and exclaiming, "Lor, but her be a booty." I thought I was not needed among so many women, so I brought Gwenny in and gave her a potful of bacon and peas and an iron spoon to eat it with, which she did right heartily.

We settled Lorna in a deep old chair with plenty of pillows and there she sat with her sad white face not seeming to take anything in and her beautiful hands spread out from time to time before the blazing fire.

"All go away except my mother," I said very quietly, but so that I would be obeyed and everybody knew it.

Mother and I sat and watched my darling, and then a little sob disturbed us, and mother tried to make believe that she was only coughing. But Lorna, guessing who she was, jumped up so quickly that she almost set her frock on fire from the great ash-log, and away she ran to the old oak chair, where mother was by the clock-case pretending to be knitting, and she knelt down humbly and gazed up at mother.

"God bless you, my fair mistress!" said mother, bending nearer, "God bless you, my sweet child!"

And so she went to mother's heart, by the very nearest road, even as she had come to mine. I mean the road of pity, smoothed by grace and youth and gentleness.

Chapter XXVI

Jeremy Stickles had gone south before the frost set in to muster forces to attack the Doone Glen. But now this weather had put a stop to every kind of movement, for even if men could have borne the cold, they could not face the perils of the snowdrifts. This meant that the Doones could not come prowling after Lorna, while the snow lay piled between us with the surface soft and dry. But putting two and two together, and having seen me at their Captain's funeral with Lorna, they would know where to come when the weather was better. Therefore I set all hands on to thresh the corn, before the Doones could come and burn the ricks.

The terrible weather lasted from the middle of December until the second week in March, and during that time Lorna became part of the family and was loved by all, even Lizzie when she found out how many books Lorna had read.

After the frost came rain and floods but it was now time to work very hard, both to make up for the farm-work lost during the months of frost and snow, and also to be ready for a great and vicious attack by the Doones, who would burn us in our beds at the earliest opportunity. Meanwhile we did what yard-work we could and took stock of our losses. The sheep and cattle had suffered dreadfully and many had died.

Now, in spite of the floods and the state of the roads most perilous, Squire Faggus came at last, riding his famous strawberry mare. There was great ado between him and Annie, as you may well suppose, after four months of parting. He told us that he had bought a piece of land to the south of the moors which would be of the very finest pasture when it got a good store of rain and he saw at once that he could breed fine cattle there.

Being such a hand as he was at making the most of everything, he had actually turned to his own advantage the extraordinary weather by teaching Winnie to go out in the snowy evenings and whinny to the forest ponies and she never came home without at least a score of hungry ponies trotting after her, tossing their heads and tails in turn and pretending to be very wild. Tom would feed them well and turn them into his great cattle-pen ready for breaking in when the frost should be over.

Tom Faggus spoke to mother and me about the time for his marriage to Annie, and we told him that Annie herself must decide. Neither mother nor I were very happy about the marriage because of Tom's past, but he had received the King's pardon, and was now a pattern of honesty.

Tom was much impressed by Lorna at supper and she treated him with the greatest courtesy. His gaze went from her beautiful face to the glass necklace several times when he was not smiling at his Annie.

Now when the young maidens were gone – for we had quite a high dinner of fashion that day, with Betty Muxworthy waiting on us and Gwenny Carfax at the gravy – and only mother and Tom and I remained at the white deal table with brandy and schnapps and hot water jugs, Squire Faggus said quite suddenly, "What do you know of the history of that beautiful maiden, good mother?"

"Not half as much as my son does," answered mother with a soft smile at me, "and when John does not choose to tell a thing, wild horses will not pull it out of him."

"That is not at all like me, mother," I replied rather sadly, "you know almost every word about Lorna, quite as well as I do." I said no more, for in truth I had not told mother a few things which might upset her, especially that I was sure Carver Doone would seek his revenge on us for taking Lorna into the care of our family.

"That necklace," said Tom, gratefully accepting another glass of brandy, "that necklace of hers is worth a fortune."

"What," said I, "that common glass thing which she has had from her childhood!"

"Glass indeed! They are the finest jewels ever I set eyes on and I have handled a good many."

"Surely," cried mother, now flushing as red as Tom's own cheeks with excitement, "you must be wrong, or the young mistress would herself have known it."

"Trust me," answered Tom, in his loftiest manner, which Annie said was "so noble", but which seemed to me rather flashy, "trust me for knowing jewels when I see them. I would have stopped an eight-horse coach with four armed outriders for such a booty as that. Those were days worth living in, but alas they are over now. I shall never know the likes again. How fine it was by moonlight!"

"Master Faggus," said my mother, in a very dignified

manner, "Annie is my eldest beloved daughter and the child of a most upright man. I will not risk my Annie's life with a man who yearns for a life of highway robbery."

Mother started to cry on my shoulder, and, but for comforting her, I would gladly have taken Tom by the nose, and thrown him, and Winnie after him, over our farmyard gate.

Chapter XXVII

Scarcely had Tom Faggus left than in came Jeremy Stickles, splashed with mud from head to foot and not in the best of tempers though happy to get back again. While Annie looked after him and saw that a meal was prepared, I went to the horse. He was blown so that he could hardly stand, and plastered with mud and steaming, so that the stable was quite full of it. By the time I had put the poor fellow to rights, his master had finished his dinner and was in a better humour. He told me that as he was riding towards us, from the town of Southmolton in Devonshire, he found the roads very soft and heavy and the floods out in all directions from the melting of the snow. He had only a single trooper with him, a man not of the militia, but of the King's army whom Jeremy had brought from Exeter. As the two descended towards the Landacre Bridge, they discovered that the flooding was so bad that only the parapets of the bridge could be seen above the water.

They decided to swim for it and Jeremy, dashing into the river, urged his horse for the bridge and gained it with some little trouble, and there he found the water not more than up to his horse's knees perhaps. On the crown of the bridge he turned his horse to watch the trooper's passage and help him with directions, when suddenly he saw him fall headlong into the torrent and heard the report of a gun from behind. Turning round he saw three men, risen up from behind the hedge on one side of the road ahead of him, two of them ready to load again and one with his gun unfired, waiting to get good aim at him. Jeremy set spurs to his horse, rode straight at the man, fired one shot and lying flat along the horse's neck galloped for his life. Looking back he saw the three men hastily mounting their horses, but he outdistanced them and finally they lost him.

When he had rested I held a council with my good friend Stickles, telling him all about Lorna's presence and what I knew of her history. He agreed with me that we could not hope to escape an attack from the outlaws, the more especially as they knew he was on his way back to Plover's Barrows when they attacked. Jeremy advised me to have all the entrances to the house strengthened, to maintain a watch at night and thought it would be wise for me to go (late as it was) to Lynmouth, if a horse could pass through the flooded valley, and fetch Sergeant Bloxham and every one of his mounted troopers who were far more use than the local militia who spent most of their time arguing among themselves. I set off, wishing that I had kept Tom Faggus with us, and made as good speed as I could through the floods, not wishing to leave the women for long.

At Lynmouth I found four troopers, but they had to come without their horses and follow but further inland so that they could cross the river further upstream.

When I returned, wet and exhausted, I found they had all waited up for me. They left me quietly with Lorna while I had my supper and went off to bed.

She came close to me, laid her head on my shoulder and said, "Can't you keep out of this fight, John?"

"My own one," I answered, "I believe there will be nothing, but whatever happens, I must see it out."

"Shall I tell you what I think, John?"

"Let us have it dear, by all means. You know so much about their ways."

"What I believe is this, John. You know how high the rivers are, higher than ever they were before, and twice as high, you have told me. I believe that Glen Doone is flooded, and all the houses under water."

"You clever little darling," I answered, "what a fool I must be not to think of it! Of course it is; it must be. The torrent from all the Bagworthy forest, and all the valleys above it, and the great snowdrifts in the glen itself, could never all find an outlet down my famous waterslide. The valley must be under twenty feet of water at least. Well, if ever there was a fool, I am he for not having thought of it."

"I remember once before" said Lorna, reckoning on her fingers, "when there was very heavy rain, all through the autumn and winter, five or it may be six years ago, the river came down with such a rush that the water was two feet deep in our rooms, and we all had to camp by the cliff edge."

"The floods are even higher now," I answered. "You may take my word for it, Mistress Lorna, that your pretty bower is six feet deep."

"Well, my bower has served its time," said Lorna, "and it is here now, John. But I am so sorry to think of all the poor women flooded out of their houses, and sheltering in

122

the snowdrifts. However, there is one good thing about it: they cannot send many men against us, with all this trouble upon them."

"You are right," I replied, "how clever you are! And that is why there were only three to cut off Mr Stickles. And now we shall beat them, I make no doubt, that is if they come at all. And I defy them to fire the house; the thatch is too wet for burning."

We sent all the women to bed quite early, except Gwenny Carfax and our good old Betty Muxworthy. These two we allowed to stay up, because they might be useful to us, if they could keep from quarelling. It was not likely that the Doones could bring more than eight or ten men against us while their homes were in such danger, and to meet these we had Sergeant Bloxham and eight good men including Jeremy and myself, all well-armed and resolute, besides our three farm workers armed with farming implements, the parish clerk and the shoemaker. John Fry had his blunderbuss, loaded with tin-tacks and marbles, and more likely to kill the man who discharged it than any other person, but we knew that John only had it for show and to show what a superior weapon it was.

I took up my post by the rick-yard, knowing that the Doones would probably begin their attack there by starting a fire, but I had not been very long waiting and listening with my best gun ready and a big club by me, before a heaviness of sleep began to creep upon me. So I leaned back in the clover-rick, thinking of my Lorna and fell fast asleep.

Chapter XXVIII

It was not likely that the outlaws would attack our premises until some time after the moon was risen, because it would be too dangerous to cross the flooded valleys in the darkness of the night. I suppose I must have realized this and that is why I allowed myself to sleep, but it was a foolish thing to do and especially foolish to do it in the rick-yard which might be set on fire by the enemy when they did come.

Luckily I was awoken by Lorna who told me that the man on guard at the back of the house was fast asleep, but that Gwenny was perched in a nearby tree which overlooked the Barrow valley up which the Doones would almost certainly come to cross the stream. Lorna thought the women should help with the watch because they were not tired with travelling, but I could not allow this and she agreed to go back into the house. However, I allowed Gwenny to stay in her tree and started patrolling the ricks and stables. Presently a short wide figure stole towards me, in and out of the shadows, and I saw that it was the little maid herself and that she had some news.

"Ten on 'em crossed the water down yonder," said Gwenny, putting her hand to her mouth and sounding quite pleased. "They be all creeping up by hedgerow now. I could shoot three on 'em from the bar gate, if I had your gun, young man."

"There is no time to lose, Gwenny. Run to the house and fetch Master Stickles and all the men, while I stay here and watch the rick-yard."

The robbers rode into our yard as coolly as if they had been invited. The gate was, of course, locked, so they took it off its hinges. I could see our troopers, waiting in the shadow of the house, round the corner from where the Doones were, and expecting the order to fire. But Jeremy Stickles very wisely kept them in readiness, until the enemy should advance upon them.

"Two of you lazy fellows go," it was the deep voice of Carver Doone, "and make us a light to cut their throats by. Only one thing, once again. If any man touches Lorna, I will stab him where he stands. She belongs to me."

Hidden in the rick I aimed my gun straight at the light buckled to his belt and yet I could not pull the trigger. Would to God that I had done so! I had never taken human life, nor caused anyone bodily harm apart from the little bruises and the trifling aches and pains which follow a good and honest bout in the wrestling ring. Therefore I dropped my gun and picked up my sturdy club.

Presently two young men came towards me carrying torches lit from Carver's lamp. I took them by surprise, laid one on the ground with a broken elbow and the other on top of him with a broken collar-bone.

Suddenly a blaze of fire lit up the house and brown

smoke hung around it. Six of our men had let go at the Doones by Jeremy Stickles' order as the villains came swaggering down in the moonlight. Two of them fell, and the rest hung back not knowing what to do. They were not used to this sort of thing. Taking advantage of this, I ran across the yard. No one shot at me and I went up to Carver Doone, whom I knew by his size in the moonlight, and I took him by the beard and said, "Do you call yourself a man?"

For a moment he was so astonished that he could not answer. No one had dared, I suppose, to look at him in that way, and he saw that he had met his equal, or perhaps his master. He pointed a pistol at me, but I was too quick for him.

"Now Carver Doone," I said quietly, "you are a fool to set yourself against me. You are also a villain. Lie low in your native muck."

And with that, I laid him flat upon his back in our straw-yard by a trick of the inner heel, which he could not have resisted (though his strength had been twice as great as mine), unless he were also a wrestler. Seeing him down, the others ran, though one of them took a shot at me, and some of them jumped on their horses, before our men could get to them, and some went away without them. And among these last was Captain Carver who got up while I was examining a small wound I had received and strode away with a stream of curses, enough to poison the light of the moon.

We gained six very good horses, two prisoners, the ones I had knocked down in the rick-yard, and there were two dead Doones. We buried them in the churchyard without a service and I was glad *I* had not killed them.

Jeremy sent for an escort for the two prisoners, whom we had roped to the cider-press, and they were marched

126

away. The women and indeed all of us felt sorry for them and we heard afterwards that they were sentenced to death at the next assizes.

Chapter XXIX

Soon after the battle of Plover's Barrows Farm, another very important matter called for our attention. This was no less than Annie's marriage to Squire Faggus. We had tried to put it off again, for in spite of all advantages, neither mother nor I had any real heart for it. We knew that he had the King's pardon and the universal respect of the neighbourhood, but we both had misgivings as to his future steadiness. He had a kind of a turn for drinking. We would discuss this, but almost always finished up by saying, "Well, well, there is no telling. No one can say how a man may change after he is married." But if we could only make Annie promise to be a little firm with him!

I fear that all this talk on our part only hurried matters forward, Annie being more determined every time we pitied her. And at last Tom Faggus came and spoke as if he was on the King's highway with a pistol at my head and one at mother's. "No more fast and loose," he cried, "either one thing or the other. I love Annie and she loves me and we will have one another, either with your leave or without it. How many more times am I to dance over these vile hills and leave my business and get nothing more than a sigh or a kiss, and, 'Tom, I must wait for mother.' You are famous for being straightforward, you Ridds. Just treat me as I would treat you, now."

I looked at my mother, for a glance from her would have sent Tom out of the window, but she checked me with her hand and said, "You have some reason to complain, sir; I will not deny it. Now I will be straightforward with you. My son and I have all along disliked the idea of your marriage to Annie. We do not fear you taking to the highway life again, but we fear that you will take to drinking and squandering money. There are many examples of this around us, and we know what the fate of the wife is. It has been hard to tell you this, under our own roof, and with our own – " Here mother hesitated.

"Spirits and cider and beer," I broke in, "out with it, mother."

"Spirits and cider and beer," said mother very firmly after me, and then she gave way and said, "You know, Tom, you are welcome to every drop, and more of it."

Now Tom must have had a far sweeter temper than ever I could claim, for I should have thrust my glass away, and never taken another drop in the house, but instead of that Master Faggus replied with a pleasant smile, "I know that I am welcome, good mother, and to prove it, I will have some more." And thereupon he mixed himself another glass of gin, with lemon and hot water, yet pouring it very delicately.

"Oh, I have been so miserable! – take a little more, Tom," said mother, handing the bottle.

"Yes, take a little more," I said, "you have mixed it

over weak, Tom."

"If ever there was in Christendom a sober man," said Tom, "that man is now before you. Shall we say tomorrow week, mother? It will suit your washing-day."

"How thoughtful you are, Tom! Now John would never have thought of that in spite of all his steadiness."

"Certainly not," I answered proudly, "when my time comes for Lorna, I shall not study Betty Muxworthy."

In this way the Squire got over us and Annie began to prepare her wedding garments and the clothes that she would wear as Mistress Faggus.

Annie's beauty and kindliness had made her the pride of the neighbourhood and the presents sent her from all around were enough to stock a shop with.

Annie and Tom were married in Oare Church with our blessing and Lorna and Lizzie did their best to take her place and cherish mother.

Chapter XXX

All our neighbourhood was surprised that the Doones had not attacked us again and probably made an end of us. After the first attack, several troopers with their sergeant had been left with us for protection and Jeremy Stickles stayed on and off for some time, but now we lay almost at their mercy, having only Sergeant Bloxham and three men to protect us, Captain Stickles having been ordered southwards with all his force except those who were needed to check goods that were coming into Lynmouth and destined for Porlock.

Now the reason why the Doones did not attack us was that they were preparing to meet a powerful assault upon their fortress by the forces of the King. And no doubt they were right, for although the disputes in government during the summer and autumn had delayed the matter, yet positive orders had been issued that these robbers and outlaws should at any price be brought to justice. But then the sudden death of King Charles II threw all things into confusion, and all minds into a panic.

We heard of it first in church on Sunday, the 8th day of February 1685. The news was brought by Sam Fry, a cousin of our John Fry, but, thinking he might perhaps share our John Fry's habit of exaggerating (to put it kindly), I decided to find out for myself if our King was really dead.

At Porlock, I found that it was too true, and the women of the town were in great distress, for the King had always been popular with them. The men on the other hand were forecasting all kinds of trouble.

Almost before we had put off our mourning clothes, which as loyal subjects we wore for the King, three months and a week, rumours of disturbances, of plottings and of trouble breaking out began to stir amongst us. We heard of fighting in Scotland, and buying of ships on the continent, and of arms in Dorset and Somerset, and we kept our beacon in readiness to give signals of a landing, or rather the soldiers did so for many had no love for sour James, such as we had for the lively Charles and feared he might try to bring back the Catholic religion.

We listened to all the rumours and shook our heads gravely. Nevertheless, in our part of the country, things went on as usual, until the middle of June was near. We ploughed the ground, and sowed the corn and tended the cattle and talked about the neighbours much as usual, and the only thing that moved us much was that Annie had a baby. He was a very fine child with blue eyes and christened John after me and I was proud to be his godfather.

For the next fortnight, we were daily troubled with conflicting rumours, each man relating what he wanted rather than what he had the right to believe, but it did seem as if a rebellion was brewing with the Duke of Monmouth, a

Protestant, the son of Charles II, but with no right to the throne, at its head.

One day at the beginning of July, I came home from mowing about noon, or a little later, to fetch some cider for all of us and to eat a morsel of bacon. For mowing was no joke that year, the summer being wonderfully wet (even for our wet country), and the swathe of grass falling heavier over the scythe than ever I can remember it. We were drenched with rain almost every day, but the mowing must be done somehow, and we must trust to God for the haymaking.

In the courtyard I saw a smart little cart and thought we had an important visitor, but behold it was no one greater than our Annie, with my godson in her arms, and looking pale and tearful.

"John, I am in such trouble," she said, wiping her eyes.

"Don't you cry, my dear, don't cry, my darling sister," I answered as she dropped into a chair and bent above her infant, rocking as if both their hearts were gone.

"But John, how can I help crying? I am in such trouble."

"Tell me what it is, my dear. Any grief of yours will vex me greatly, but I will try to bear it."

"Then, John, it is just this. Tom has gone off with the Duke of Monmouth's rebels, and you must, oh you must, go after him."

Chapter XXXI

For the sake of the safety of Lorna and mother and Lizzie and the rest of the household, I would have been obliged to refuse Annie's plea, had I not heard that the Doones had thrown in their lot with the Duke of Monmouth and most of them had joined the rebels. Even so, I was uneasy, but I was moved by Annie's tears and when she promised to stay and look after things, I said I would go.

Right early in the morning, I was off without a word to anyone, not even Lorna, fearing a scene and knowing that all the women had cried themselves to sleep the night before. John Fry was left with the hay crop and I took my horse Kickums, who, although true to his name, was better than ten sweet-tempered horses. It seemed to me to be a wild goose chase and I did not know where the Duke of Monmouth's army was or if it was moving from place to place.

We rattled away at a merry pace and made for Dulverton where we both fed and rested. Then we set off across the moorland until we came to a town and there made enquiries and so on to the next and most of the time it was false information or I had to go out of my way to avoid the King's soldiers because I was seeking the rebels although my own loyalty was to the King. In succession I was sent to Bath, Frome, Wells, Wincanton, Glastonbury, Shepton, Bradford, Axbridge, Somerton and Bridgewater.

This last place I reached on a Sunday night, the fourth or fifth of July, I think. Kickums and I were glad to come to a decent place, where meat and corn could be had for money, and, being quite weary of wandering about, we hoped to rest there a little.

Of this, however, we found no chance, for the town was full of the Duke of Monmouth's soldiers, if men may be called so, the half of whom had never been drilled nor had fired a gun. And it was rumoured among them that the "popish army" as they called it, meaning King James's army, was to be attacked that very night and with God's assistance beaten. However, by this time I had learnt to pay little attention to rumours, and having sought vainly for Tom Faggus, among these poor rustic warriors, I went to my hostel, and went to bed being as weary as weary can be.

I lay in the depths of deepest slumber for several hours until I was awakened by lights and noises. Through the window I could hear the distant roll of musketry and the beating of drums, with a quick rub-a-dub and the sound of the trumpet call. Perhaps Tom Faggus might be there and shot at any moment, and my dear Annie left a poor widow and my godson Jack an orphan.

I arose quickly and dressed myself, and went and woke Kickums who was snoring and set out to see the worst of it. The sleepy ostler scratched his head and could not tell me which way to take; what did he care who was King or Pope, as long as he paid his way and got a bit of bacon on Sunday?

I was guided mainly by the sounds of guns and trumpets in riding out of the narrow ways and into the open marshes. Fog came down so that, although we could hear the sounds of conflict, we could not get to it. What chance had Kickums and I, both unused to marsh and mere?

At last, when I almost despaired of escaping from this tangle of spongy banks, and of hazy creeks and reed-fringe, my horse heard the neigh of a fellow-horse, and was only too glad to answer it; upon which the other, having lost his rider, came up and pricked his ears at us and gazed at us through the fog. I whistled to him, but he capered away with his tail set on high, and the stirrup irons clashing under him. We followed him and he led us to a little hamlet, called (as I found afterwards) West Zuyland or Zealand, so named perhaps from its situation amid this inland sea.

Here the King's troops had been quite lately, and their fires were still burning, but the men themselves had been summoned away by the night attack of the rebels. However, I found for a guide a man who knew the district thoroughly, and who led me by many intricate ways to the rear of the rebel army. We came upon a broad open moor, striped with sullen watercourses, shagged with sedge, and yellow iris, and in the drier part with bilberries. By this time it was four o'clock, and the summer sun, arising wanly, showed us all the ghastly scene.

If a plain man saw what I saw that morning, the battle-field strewn with wounded and dying and corpses too many to count, he would have sickened of all desire to be great among all mankind.

Seeing me riding to the front where fighting was still

going on, fugitives called to me to make no utter fool of myself, for the great guns had come, and the fight was over. All the rest was slaughter.

"All up wi' Monmouth," shouted one big fellow, a miner of the Mendip hills, whose weapon was a pickaxe. "Na use to fight na more. Wend thee home, young man, again."

Hearing this, I stopped my horse, desiring not to be shot for nothing and eager to aid some poor wounded people who tried to lift their arms to me. I did the best I could for them, though not skilled in this kind of thing and more inclined to weep with them than check their weeping. While I was giving a drink to one poor fellow whose life was ebbing away, I felt warm lips laid against my cheek quite softly, and then a little push, and behold it was a horse leaning over me! I arose in haste and there stood Tom's horse Winnie, looking at me with beseeching eyes, enough to melt a heart of stone. Seeing that she had my attention, she turned her head, and glanced back sadly towards the place of battle and gave a little wistful neigh, and then looked me full in the face again, as much as to say, "Do you understand?" while she scraped with one hoof impatiently. If ever a horse tried hard to speak, it was Winnie at that moment. I went to her side and patted her, but that was not what she wanted. Then I offered to leap into the empty saddle, but that was not right either, for she ran away towards the part of the field, at which she had been glancing back, and then turned round and shook her mane, entreating me to follow her.

The dying man was now unconscious and so, commending him to God, I mounted my own horse again much to Winnie's delight and she gave her ringing silvery neigh.

The cannons were still firing and one ball came very near

us, missing her off hind-foot by an inch and scattering black mud over Winnie, but I was more frightened than she was, and she led me forward, turning her head from time to time to make sure I was following.

Suddenly the cavalry of the King, with their horses at full speed, dashed from either side upon the helpless mob of countrymen, some only armed with scythes, pickaxes, blacksmiths' hammers or other implements. A few pikes met the soldiers, but they shot the pike-men, drew swords and leaped into the shattered and scattering mass. Right and left, they hacked and hewed. I could hear the snapping of scythes beneath them, and see the flash of their sweeping swords. How it would all end was plain enough, even to one like myself, who had never beheld such a battle before. But Winnie led me away to the left, and, as I could not help the people, neither stop the slaughter and thought myself in considerable danger, I was only too glad to follow her.

Winnie stopped in front of a low black shed, and here she uttered a little greeting, in a subdued and softened voice, hoping to obtain an answer. Receiving no reply, she entered and I leaped from Kickums' back and followed. There I found her sniffing gently at the body of Tom Faggus. I thought he was dead, but Winnie bent her head and felt him with her under lip, passing it over his skin as softly as a mother would do to an infant, and then she looked up at me again, as if to say, "He is all right."

Upon this I took courage, and handled poor Tom, which, being young, I had feared at first to do. He groaned very feebly, as I raised him up and saw that he had a deep wound in his right side. I bound this up with some of my linen to try and stop the bleeding until we could get a doctor. Then I gave him a little weak brandy and water, not really knowing if I should have given him water only, but he seemed a little better, some colour coming into his cheeks and he looked at Winnie and knew her. With the help of my arm he sat upright and managed to whisper, "Is Winnie hurt?"

"No," I replied, "she is as right as rain."

"Then so am I," said Tom. "Put me upon her back, John. She and I will find our way home together."

Knowing Tom so well and seeing that he was determined, I did what his feeble eyes sometimes implored and sometimes commanded. With a strong sash, from his own hot neck, bound and twisted tight around his damaged waist, I set him upon Winnie's back, and placed his trembling feet in stirrups, with a band from one to the other, under Winnie's body, so that no swerve could throw him out, and then I said, "Lean forward, Tom, it will stop your wound from bleeding." He leaned forward almost on the neck of the mare, which, as I knew, must close the wound. His eyes lit up and the pain eased from his face as he felt the strength of his good mare under him.

"God bless you, John, I am safe," he whispered. "Who can come near my Winnie mare? A mile of her gallop is ten years of life. Look out for yourself, John Ridd." He clicked his tongue and the mare went off as easy and swift as a swallow.

Kickums and I were worn out, so I left him cropping what grass there was, went into the hut, lay down and, in spite of the danger, fell into a deep sleep.

Chapter XXXII

I slept for three hours and was awoken by a familiar voice. Captain Jeremy Stickles, as he now was, of the King's Army limped in with a bandaged leg, wrung my hand and asked how I had come to be in such a dangerous place. "For," said he, "looking as you do, you could be mistaken for a rebel, condemned and hung on the spot by that rogue Colonel Kirke, without waiting for the next assizes when Judge Jeffreys, the Lord Chief Justice, will surely condemn many more." I shivered at the memory of that terrible man and was glad I had Captain Stickles who would speak for me if I were arrested.

I explained about Tom Faggus and that I was in honour bound to look for him for the sake of my sister Annie. Master Stickles whose wound was paining him said that he must have some rest and he offered to escort me home accompanied by a couple of troopers whom he had left standing guard outside the hut. This I gladly accepted and thought with longing of Plover's Barrows, of Lorna, Mother, Annie and Lizzie all watching and waiting and I prayed that they might be safe and that Kickums and I might travel safely back to them and that Tom Faggus might survive. Jeremy said that, apart from resting, it would suit him well to find out, on behalf of the King, what the Doones were doing and which of them had fought for the traitor Monmouth. So we set out.

When we returned home, to everyone's relief including mine, we found that good Tom Faggus was home again with his Annie and his little son Jack, and intended to go no more to war, but to look after his family.

The Doones were quiet for the moment, but this Colonel Kirke, in the most outrageous manner, had hanged no less than six of them who were captured among the rebels. This hanging of so many Doones caused some indignation among people who were used to them, and it seemed for a while to depress the spirits of many of the local people.

The women tended Captain Stickles and made a great fuss of him and I worked on the farm and tried to find out what John Fry and the other men had done or not done, but in the evenings I sat thankfully with my dear ones with my Lorna in pride of place with her little hand in mine and her beautiful eyes aglow with love.

Chapter XXXIII

I was sitting one evening with Jeremy, who was not yet well enough to return to the army, having a quiet drink and smoking our pipes as the women had gone to bed.

I thought this might be my chance to share my thoughts with him about something which had puzzled me for some time. This was the mystery of Lorna's necklace, since, according to Tom Faggus, it was made not of glass beads but of precious stones. The Doones were known to have lost all their property and, if it was stolen, surely they would have sold it for a good sum of money.

"You are speaking to the right man," said Jeremy. "I have been of a mind to tell you something of Lady Lorna, for I believe we do not know the truth about her."

"What do you know that I do not know?" I said and something stirred in my heart and my hand shook as I held my glass. "Tell me at once."

"Calm yourself, John, said Master Stickles, "and I will tell you a story."

I tried to appear calm and he started:

"It was several months ago, at any rate a good while before that cursed frost began, the mere name of which sends a shiver down every bone of my body, when I was riding one afternoon from Dulverton to Watchett. It was near evening, and I was getting weary. The road (if road it could be called) turned suddenly down from the higher land to the very brink of the sea, and rounding a little jut of cliff, I met the roar of the breakers. My horse was scared and leaped aside, for a northerly wind was piping and driving hunks of foam across, as children scatter snowballs. But he only sank to his fetlocks in the dry sand, and I tried to make him face the waves, and then I looked about me.

"Watchett town was not to be seen, on account of a little foreland, a mile or more upon my course, and standing to the right of me. There was room enough below the cliffs for horse and man to get along, although the tide was running high with a northerly gale to back it. But close at hand and in a corner, drawn above the yellow sands and long eyebrows of seaweed, as snug a little house blinked on me as ever I saw, or wished to see. It was a little inn and I thought to myself how snug it was and how beautifully I could sleep there. I turned the old horse towards it, which he was only too glad to do, and we climbed above the spring-tide mark, and over a little piece of turf and knocked on the door. Someone came and peeped at me through the glass above, and then the bolt was drawn back and a woman met me very courteously. She was a dark and foreign-looking woman and she waited for me to speak first which an Englishwoman would not have done.

"'Can I rest here for the night?' I asked, lifting my hat to

143

her, 'my horse is weary and I am but little better; besides that we are both famished.'

"'Yes sir, you can rest and welcome. As for food, I am afraid there is only bacon and eggs.'

"'Bacon!' said I, 'what can be better? And half a dozen eggs with it, and a quart of fresh-drawn ale.' The woman called a little maid to lead my horse to stable. However, I preferred to see to him myself and told her to send the little maid for the frying pan and the egg-box.

"I began to wonder how such a handsome woman could have settled in this lonely inn with only the waves for company and a very ordinary (as she later told me) husband who slaved all day turning a potter's wheel at Watchett.

"However, I did not have to wonder very long, for when she found out who I was, and how I held the King's commission and might be called an officer, she seemed pleased to tell me her story.

"Her name was Benita and she was an Italian from the mountains of Apulia, who had gone to Rome to seek her fortune, after being badly treated in some love affair. She found employment in a large hotel and, rising gradually, began to send money to her parents. While working in the hotel, she met a rich and noble English family who took a liking to her and asked her to take service with them and look after their children. Benita had grown to love the children and so she accepted the position.

"At first everything went well. They travelled through Northern Italy, and throughout the south of France and were as happy as could be. The children (a girl and a boy) laughed and grew and thrived, especially the young lady who was the elder of the two.

"My Lord, who was quite a young man still, rode on one day in front of his wife and friends to catch the first of

144

a famous view on the French side of the Pyrenees. He kissed his hand to his wife and said that he would save her the trouble of coming. They were a devoted couple and understood each other well. And so off went my Lord ahead with a fine young horse leaping up at every step. He rode wildly and his wife feared for him.

"They waited for him long and long, but he never came back and within a week his mangled body lay in a little chapel-yard and his poor wife, who was expecting another child, knew herself a widow.

"My Lady stayed for six months more, scarcely able to believe that all her fright was not a dream, but at the end of October, when wolves come down to the farm-lands, the little family went home to England and Benita went with them.

"They landed somewhere on the Devonshire coast, ten or eleven years ago, and stayed some days at Exeter, and from there set out in a hired coach, without any proper attendance, for Watchett in the north of Somerset where the lady owned a quiet mansion just outside the town.

"The weather was atrocious, but through fog and through muck the coach went on as best it could until dark, but when they came to the pitch and slope of the sea-bank, leading on towards Watchett town, where my horse had shied so, the little boy jumped up and clapped his hands at the water, and there (as Benita said) they met their fate.

"Although it was past the dusk of day, the silver light from the sea flowed in, and showed the cliffs, and the grey sand-line, and the drifts of seaweed. It showed them also a troop of horsemen, waiting under a rock hard by and ready to dash upon them. The postilions drove the horses towards the sea to try and escape and the serving-men cocked their blunderbusses, while my Lady stood up bravely in the carriage and hid her son behind her. Meanwhile the drivers drove into the sea, till the leading horses were swimming.

"But before the waves came into the coach, a score of fierce men were round it. They cursed the postilions for mad cowards, and cut the traces, and seized the wheel-horses who were all wild with dismay in the wet and the dark. Benita, realizing that all their boxes would be turned inside out or carried away, snatched the most valuable of the jewels, a magnificent necklace of diamonds, cast it over the little girl's head, and buried it under her travelling-cloak, hoping by that means to save it. Then a great wave, crested with foam, rolled in, and the coach was thrown on its side, and the sea rushed in at the top and the windows and Benita fainted away.

"When she recovered her senses, she found herself upon the sand, the robbers were out of sight, and one of the serving-men was bathing her forehead with sea-water. She got up and ran to her mistress who was sitting upright on a little rock, with her dead boy's face to her bosom, sometimes gazing upon him, and sometimes looking round for her little girl.

"Before the light of the morning came along the tide to Watchett, my Lady had met her husband in heaven. They took her into the town that night and there her baby was born and soon after they both died. The Lady lies in Watchett churchyard, with her son and heir at her right hand, and a tiny baby, of sex unknown, sleeping on her bosom."

"What was the lady's name?" I asked, "and what became of the little girl? And why did the woman stay there?"

"Well," said Jeremy, "to take the last first: Benita stayed in that blessed place, because she could not get away from it. The Doones – if Doones indeed they were – took everything out of the carriage, wet or dry they took it. And Benita could never get her wages for the whole affair is in the Court of Chancery now."

"Whew!" said I, knowing something of London, and not thinking much of Benita's chances.

"So the poor thing was compelled to drop all thought of Apulia, and settle down on the brink of Exmoor. She married a man who turned a wheel for making that blue Watchett ware. He had a house and there they are with their three children and there you may go and visit them."

"And what became of the little maid?"

"You are rather more likely to know," said Jeremy, "than anyone. As certain sure as I stand here, that little maid is Lorna Doone."

Chapter XXXIV

Jeremy's tale moved me greatly and, the more I thought about it, the more I became convinced that the child of those unlucky parents was indeed my Lorna. If that was so, I should have to tell her and the Court of Chancery would have to confirm her heritage. However, first I must go and see Benita at Watchett to confirm the story Jeremy had told me and to find out the name of the parents. Jeremy, for reasons of his own, had not told me this. Indeed I was half afraid to know it, remembering that the nobler and the wealthier she proved to be, the smaller was my chance of winning such a wife for plain John Ridd. Not that she would give me up, that I never dreamed of, but that others might interfere, or indeed that I myself might find it only honest to give her up. That last thought was a dreadful blow and I tried not to think about it.

A few days later, and before I could get to Watchett, by some coincidence two fellows arrived bearing messages from London. The Court of Chancery, having a power of scent better than a tracker dog, had traced Lorna to our farm, having first visited the Doones. They bore two documents. One was addressed to Mistress Lorna Doone, so called, bidding her keep in readiness to travel when called upon, and to go only with the messengers of the right honourable court, while the other was addressed to all subjects of His Majesty, having custody of Lorna Doone, a young lady of under twenty-one years, to yield her up to the Court.

My mother and I discussed these writs, as I believe they are called, with a mixture of anger and fear and agreed that Lorna must be told at once.

I found Lorna in a little garden she had made, asked her to sit down and told her the whole story. She was in tears when I had finished, thinking of the tragic fate of her father, mother and little brother.

"Dearest," I said, "you must keep your proper dignity. I am far below you now."

"Are you saying that you want to give me up?" she asked in a voice which trembled.

"Sweetest of all sweet loves, what could ever make me give up my Lorna?"

"Dearest of all dears," she answered, "what could ever make me give you up, dear?"

Upon that I kissed and clasped her, whether she were Lady, Countess or Queen of England, mine she was at least in heart, and mine she should be wholly.

We sat silently for a while on a little bench and finally she said, "So I am not a Doone?"

"You are not a Doone, my Lorna, but I do not yet know your name."

She fell silent, trying to take this all in and then I said, "I am going to see the nursemaid who was with you. She will tell me your real name."

"How can it matter to me, John?" she answered sadly. "It can never matter now when there are none to share it."

"Poor little soul!" was all I said, in a tone of purest pity, and, to my surprise, she turned to me, caught me in her arms and cried, "Dearest, I have you and now that is all that matters."

We sent the messengers of Chancery back to London promising that we would communicate with the Court in due course and rather hoping that with all the troubles in the country, Lorna's case might be forgotten awhile. As soon as I could, I went to see Benita. She told me that Lorna's parents were the Earl and Countess of Dugal and that therefore Lorna's name was Lady Lorna Dugal. This information meant little to Lorna, but she begged me to take her to see her old nurse, so I went back with Lorna and, pretending I wanted to go for a walk, left them together for a while in their happiness.

Chapter XXXV

And now the Doones began to plague the countryside again, and their greed and arrogance and tyranny knew no bounds. It was extraordinary that the people put up with it for so long. Whatever they wanted, they demanded and got and yet they were continually complaining. The final outrage was the carrying off of two maidens in our neighbourhood, one of whom had been at school with me before I went to Blundell's.

We had had enough, and since no one would come to our aid, we decided to deal with the Doones once and for all.

The people came flocking all around me, at the blacksmith's forge, and the Brendon ale-house, and I could scarce come out of church, but they got me among the tombstones. They all agreed that I was their natural leader. I told them to go to the magistrates, but they said that they had been often and nothing had come of it, now they must fight their cause themselves.

"Try to lead us," they said, "and we will try not to run away."

At last I agreed to this; that if the Doones, upon fair challenge, would not return our two girls, then I would lead an expedition, and do my best to subdue them. All our men were content with this, knowing from experience that the haughty robbers would only shoot any man who dared approach them individually with such a proposal.

And then arose a difficult question – who was willing to take the risk of calling on the Doones? I waited for the rest to offer, and, as none was ready, the burden fell on me. I said I would go and, after all, it had been my suggestion in the first place.

It may have been three of the afternoon, when leaving my witnesses behind (for they preferred the background), I appeared with our Lizzie's white handkerchief upon a long stick, at the entrance to the robbers' dwelling. I took no weapons since mine was a peaceful mission. Presently two decent Doones appeared and, hearing the purpose of my visit, offered to go and fetch the Captain, if I would stop where I was and not go spying around. To this, of course, I agreed at once as I already knew the ins and outs of the place.

The two men came back in a little while with a sharp short message that Captain Carver would come out and speak to me, by-and-by when his pipe was finished. I waited a long time until at length a heavy and haughty step sounded along the stone roof of the passage, and then the great Carver Doone drew up and looked at me rather scornfully.

"What is it you want, young man?" he asked as if he had never seen me before.

In spite of the strong loathing which I have always felt

at the sight of him, I kept my temper and told him that I had come for his good and that of his band. That a feeling of indignation had arisen among us about the recent behaviour of certain young men, for which perhaps he was not responsible, but I begged him clearly to understand that a vile action had taken place which we would not put up with, but that if he restored our two maidens to us, we would overlook it and things could go on as usual.

Carver made me a mocking bow and asked how I could complain of Doones carrying away maidens when I had secretly taken their little Queen from them.

To this I replied, "I took your Queen because you starved her, having stolen her long before, and killed her mother and brother. This is not for me to dwell upon now, any more than I would say much about your murdering of my father. But how the balance hangs between us, God knows better than you or I, you low villain, Carver Doone."

"I always wish to do my best, John Ridd, with the worst people who come near me. And of all I have ever met with, you are the worst of all." I did my best to look calmly at him, and said with a quiet voice, "Farewell Carver Doone, this time; our day of reckoning will be soon."

"You fool, it has come already," he cried, leaping aside into the niche of rock by the doorway. "Fire!"

The word "Fire!" was scarcely out of his mouth when I was out of fire by a single bound behind the rocky pillar of the opening. I could see the muzzles of the guns trained on me from the darkness of the cavern, but I was so quick that the men could not check their fingers crooked upon the heavy triggers and the volley sang with a roar behind it, down the avenue of crags. I turned and ran at top speed away from these vile fellows, and luckily for me, they had no more shot to send after me. And thus, by good fortune, I escaped, but with a bitter heart and mind at their unspeakable treachery.

Without any further hesitation, I agreed to take command of the honest men who were burning to punish or even destroy the outlaws as their deeds could not be borne any more.

We assembled as many men as we could and started on a plan of campaign. Recruits from round about joined us, including several of the yeomanry from Barnstaple and from Tiverton. They had heavy swords and short carbines and their appearance was truly formidable. Tom Faggus also joined us heartily, being now quite healed of his wound, except at times when the wind was easterly, and he was made second in command.

Tom Faggus devised a clever plan and this was to lure some of the Doones from their fortress by spreading it about that there was a vast sum of money including gold hidden in some old mine workings nearby. Simon Carfax, the father of Gwenny, who had recently come from Cornwall and actually was a miner himself, was to offer to guide them for the sake of a quarter share. He would advise them to send at least twenty men and at some stage when it was dark would contrive to pour a little water into the priming of their guns. It was a dangerous mission and we had to bribe him to undertake it. Also, of course, he was beholden to me for rescuing his Gwenny from the Doones and giving her a home.

Chapter XXXVI

Having resolved on a night assault (as our untrained men, three-fourths of whom had never been shot at, could not fairly be expected to march up to visible musket mouths), we did not bother much about drilling our forces, only to teach them to hold a musket and to make them familiar with the noise it made in exploding. And we fixed upon Friday night for our venture, because the moon would be at the full, and our powder was coming from Dulverton on the Friday afternoon.

It was settled that the yeomen, having good horses under them, and some strong local miners should deal with as many of the Doones who were sent to plunder the hidden treasure (as they thought). And as soon as we knew that this party of robbers was out of hearing from the valley, we would pretend to attack the Doone-gate (which was impregnable now), but the main thrust would really be to their rear, by means of my old waterslide. For I had chosen twenty young fellows, some other miners, and warehousemen and sheep-farmers, and some with other occupations, but all to be relied upon for courage and power of climbing. And with proper tools to help us and myself to lead the way, I was sure we could reach the crest, where first I had met with Lorna. I felt sorry for her because, whatever her feelings about them, we were going to try and destroy the people she had grown up with, but all of us were resolved to have no more shilly-shallying, but to go through with a nasty business, in the style of honest Englishmen, when the question comes to "Your life or mine."

The moon was lifting well above the shoulder of the uplands, when we, the chosen band, set forth, taking the short cut along the valleys to the foot of the Bagworthy water. Having allowed the rest of an hour to get round the moors and hills, we were not to begin our climbing until we heard a musket fired from the heights, on the left hand side, where John Fry himself was stationed, upon his own, at his wife's request, to keep him out of combat. And that was the place where I had been used to sit and watch for Lorna. John Fry was to fire his gun, with a ball of wool inside it, as soon as he heard the hurly-burly at the Doone-gate beginning, which we, by reason of the waterfall, could not hear down in the meadows there.

We waited a very long time, and then suddenly the most awful noise that anything short of thunder could make, came down among the rocks and hung around the corners.

"The signal, my lads!" I cried, leaping up, "now hold on by the rope, and lay your quarter-staffs across, and keep your guns pointing to heaven, lest by mistake we shoot each other. Remember, all lean well forward. If any man throws his weight back, down he will go, and perhaps he will not be able to get up again, and most likely he will shoot himself."

However, thank God, though a gun went off, no one was any the worse for it, neither did the Doones notice it, in the thick of the firing in front of them. For the order to those making the sham attack led by Tom Faggus, was to make the greatest possible noise, without coming under fire, until we in the rear had begun our attack and when this happened, John Fry would again make a signal.

Therefore we, of the chosen band, having successfully climbed the waterfall, stole up the meadow quietly, keeping in the shady bits and hollow of the water-course. And the earliest notice the Counsellor or anyone else had of our presence, was the blazing of the log-wood house where lived that villain Carver. It was my especial privilege to set this house on fire. I had insisted on it and had made all preparations carefully for a good blaze. And I must confess that I rubbed my hands, with a strong delight and comfort, when I saw the home of that man, who had fired so many houses, having its turn of smoke and blaze, and of crackling fury.

We took good care, however, to burn no women or children, for we brought them all out beforehand. Some were glad and some were sorry, according to their natures. For Carver had ten or a dozen wives, and perhaps that had something to do with his taking the loss of Lorna so easily. One child I noticed, as I saved him, a handsome little fellow, beloved by Carver Doone, as much as he could love anybody apart from himself. The boy climbed on my back and rode, and much as I hated his father, it was not in my heart to say or do a thing to upset him.

We set fire to three other houses, after calling the women to come out and telling them to go for their husbands, to come and fight a hundred of us. In the smoke, and rush, and fire, they believed that we really were a hundred, and away they ran to the battle at the Doone-gate.

"All Doone town is on fire, on fire!" we heard them shrieking as they went. "A hundred soldiers are burning it, with a dreadful great man at the head of them."

Presently, just as I expected, back came the warriors of the Doones, leaving but two or three at the gate, and burning with rage to crush under foot the invaders in their valley. It was a fine sight to see those haughty men striding down the causeway darkly, reckless of their end, but determined to have two lives for every one. A finer dozen of young men could not have been found in the world perhaps, nor a braver, nor a viler one.

Seeing how few there were of them, I did not want to fire, although I covered the leader with my gun. They were at an easy distance now, brightly shown up by the fire-light, yet not knowing where to look for us, for we had withdrawn into some bushes beneath the cliff. I thought that we might take them prisoners – though what good that would be, God knows, for they would certainly have been hanged later.

But my followers waited for no command from me. They saw a fair shot at the men they loathed, the men who had robbed them of home or of love and the chance was too good to be missed. One of the older men levelled his own gun first, a dozen muskets were discharged, and half of the Doones dropped lifeless, like so many logs of firewood.

Although I had seen a great battle before, and a hundred times the slaughter, this appeared to me to be horrible, and I was at first inclined to condemn our men for behaving so. But one instant showed me that they were right, for while the valley was filled with howling, and with shrieks of women, and the beams of blazing houses fell, and hissed in the bubbling river, all the rest of the Doones leaped at us, like so many demons. They fired wildly, not seeing us well among the hazel bushes and then they used their empty muskets as clubs or drew their swords and furiously drove at us.

For a moment, although we were twice their number, we fell back and I held my hand as long as I could, for I was waiting to fight Carver, and he was not among them. But then we attacked in force and before the daylight broke upon that ghastly March morning, the only Doones still left alive were the Counsellor and Carver. And of all the dwellings of the Doones, not even one was left, but all crumbled into potash in the river.

In these my latter years, I have often thought we took a terrible revenge on them and that I as the leader must account for it to God. And may He judge me as He knows best and may He have mercy on their souls.

Chapter XXXVII

Winning our battle produced some problems. We were afraid of being punished, either by the Justices of the Peace or even by Lord Jeffreys, who was now Lord Chancellor. We resolved this difficulty by sending all the booty taken from the Doones to the Exchequer at Westminster and let all claimants send their bills there. I have reason to believe, although this was not my intention, that Lord Jeffreys being now head of the law, and almost head of the kingdom, got possession of that money and was kindly pleased with it.

Next, with regard to the women and children, we were long in a state of perplexity. We did our very best at the farm, and so did many others, to provide for them as long as they needed help. And after a while, this trouble went, as nearly all troubles go with time. Some of the women were taken back by their parents, or their husbands, or it may be their old sweethearts, and those who failed in this, went out, some upon their own account to the New World plantations, where the fairer sex is valuable, and some to English cities, and the plainer ones to field-work. And most of the children went with their mothers, or became apprentices; only Carver Doone's handsome child had lost his mother (Carver's legal wife), and stayed with me.

This boy went about with me everywhere. He liked me as much as his father hated me, and I became almost as fond of Ensie as he was of me. He told us that his name was Ensie, short for Ensor I suppose, from his father's grandfather, the old Sir Ensor Doone.

However, although I loved the poor child, I could not help feeling very uneasy about the escape of his father, the savage and brutal Carver. This man was left to roam the country, homeless, foodless and desperate, with his giant strength, and great skill in arms, and the whole world to be revenged upon. His father Counsellor Doone was also missing and God knows what became of him. Carver had been with the party lured by Simon Carfax to the disused mine shaft to look for treasure. They got drunk in an old house nearby on spirits brought in by the miners and there they were ambushed by our men. They rushed to their guns at once, but Simon, as previously planned, had primed them with water from an old well in the courtyard and they would not fire. They fought bravely, however, and died in the hall of the old house which, by an odd coincidence had belonged to a man they had murdered. Carver Doone alone escaped. Partly through his fearful strength, and his yet more fearful face, but mainly perhaps through his perfect coolness and his way of taking things.

It had cost us sixteen men to be rid of nearly forty Doones, some in the valley and others at the old house near the mine, but for Lorna's sake I was angry that Carver

161

had escaped. According to some, he had ridden home and found all the houses ablaze. Now he swore the deadliest of oaths and seeing himself to be beaten (for the moment anyhow), he mounted his great black horse and galloped away into the darkness.

Chapter XXXVIII

A few weeks later, Lorna came of age and Jeremy and I took her to London, with Gwenny in attendance, to the Court of Chancery, whose summons she had previously disregarded. There we were told that the Lady Lorna Dugal, only surviving child of the Earl and Countess of Dugal, being now twenty-one years of age, was no longer a ward of court, but had come into her inheritance, and could marry whom she liked.

To my astonishment, while we were in London, a message came for me from the Royal Court desiring me to attend on His Majesty King James II and his Queen. The Lady Lorna Dugal was also requested to attend, so that she could be presented on her Coming of Age.

Lorna received a gracious welcome from the King and Queen, who seemed to know her sad story. Then I stepped forward and made my bow. I was told to advance and kneel down and His Majesty came down from his throne and knighted me. I thus became Sir John Ridd. I was at a loss to know why this was, but was told later that it was for keeping our part of the country loyal to the King at the time of Monmouth's rebellion and for destroying the Doones who had joined his cause and had, for many years, ravaged the countryside.

So we returned home and mother cried with joy and even Lizzie was impressed and we went straight to Parson Bowden to plan the wedding of the Lady Lorna Dugal and Sir John Ridd.

There was, in all the country round, great excitement when our plans were announced. We heard that people meant to come from more than thirty miles around, upon the excuse of seeing what a big fellow I was and hearing of the beauty of Lorna, but, in good truth, it was really curiosity and the desire to be part of a special happening.

Mother arranged all the ins and outs of the way the wedding should be done and then our day came.

Lorna's dress was of pure white, clouded with faint lavender, and as simple as need be except for loveliness. It is impossible for any, who have not loved as I have, to imagine my joy and pride, when after ring and all was done, Lorna turned to look at me. Her eyes which none on earth may ever equal, or compare with, told me such a tale of hope, and faith, and heart's devotion, that I was almost amazed, thoroughly as I knew them. Darling eyes, the clearest eyes, the loveliest, the most loving eyes – the sound of a shot rang through the church, and those eyes were dim with death.

Lorna fell across my knees, and a flood of blood came out upon the yellow wood of the altar steps, and at my feet lay Lorna, trying to tell me some last message out of her faithful eyes. I lifted her up and tried to rouse her, but it was no good, the only sign of life remaining was a drip of bright red blood. I laid my wife in my mother's arms and went forth for my revenge.

Of course, I knew who had done it. There was but one man upon earth who could have done such a thing. I leaped upon our best horse, with bridle but no saddle, and set the head of Kickums towards the course now pointed out to me. Who showed me the course, I cannot tell. I only know that I took it. And the men fell back before me.

With my vicious horse at a furious speed, I came upon Black Barrow Down, directed by some shout of men, which seemed to me but a whisper. And there, about a furlong before me, rode a man on a great black horse, and I knew that the man was Carver Doone.

"Your life or mine," I said to myself, "as the will of God may be. But we two live not upon this earth, one more hour, together."

I knew the strength of this man and I knew that he was armed with a gun — if he had time to load again, after shooting my Lorna — or at any rate with pistols, and a horseman's sword as well. I was unarmed; nevertheless, I had no doubt of killing the man before me.

I followed him over the long moor, reckless whether seen or not. But only once, the other man turned round and looked back again, and then I was beside a rock, with a seedy swamp behind me.

Although he was so far before me, and riding as hard as ride he might, I saw that he had something on the horse in front of him, something which needed care, and stopped him from looking backward.

The man turned up the gully leading from the moor to Cloven Rocks. But as Carver entered it, he turned round and beheld me not a hundred yards behind, and I saw that he was bearing his child, little Ensie, before him. Ensie also saw me, and stretched his hands and cried to me, for the face of his father frightened him.

Carver Doone, with a vile oath, urged on his tired horse and laid one hand on his pistol-stock, so that I knew he had no bullet for his gun. Kickums was as fresh as ever, and I knew that the black horse in front, if he got to the top of the steep ascent, where the track divided, must be in our reach at once.

His rider knew this, and, having no room in the rocky channel to turn and fire, drew rein at the crossways sharply, and plunged into the black ravine which led to a horrible bog.

I followed my enemy carefully, steadily, even slowly, for I had him and he could not escape. He thought that I feared to approach him, for he did not know where he was and his low, disdainful laugh came back to me. "Laugh he who wins," thought I.

An ancient and half-rotten oak hung from the crag above me. Rising from my horse's back, although I had no stirrups, I caught a branch, and tore it from the socket. Men show the rent even now, with wonder, none with more wonder than myself.

Carver Doone turned the corner suddenly on the black and bottomless bog; with a start of fear he reined back his horse, and I thought he was going to rush upon me. But instead of that, he again rode on, hoping to find a way round the side.

Now there is a way between cliff and bog, for those who know the ground thoroughly, or have time enough to search it, but for him there was no road, and he lost some time in seeking it. Upon this he made up his mind, and wheeling round, fired, and then rode at me.

His bullet struck me somewhere, but I took no heed of that. Fearing only his escape, I placed my horse across his way and with the branch of oak, brought horse and rider to the ground. Before he could slash me with his sword, he and his horse rolled over and very nearly brought my own horse down with them.

Carver Doone was somewhat stunned, and could not get up for a moment. Meanwhile I leaped on the ground, and waited, smoothing my hair back, and baring my arms, as though in the ring for wrestling. Then the little boy ran to me, clasped my leg, and looked up at me with terror in his eyes.

"Ensie dear," I said quite gently, grieving that he should see his wicked father killed, "run up there round the corner, and try to find a bunch of bluebells for the pretty lady." Ensie obeyed me while I prepared for business. There and then, I might have killed my enemy, with a single blow, while he lay unconscious, but it would have been foul play.

With a sullen scowl, Carver gathered his mighty limbs, got up and looked around for his weapons, but I had put them well away. Then he came to me and stared into my face, being accustomed to frighten young men this way.

"I would not harm you, lad," he said, with a lofty style of sneering.

"I have punished you enough for your impertinence, though not as badly as I punished your father. For the rest I forgive you, because you have been good and gracious to my little son. Go, and be contented."

For answer, I smote him on the cheek, lightly, and not to hurt him, but to make his blood leap up. I would not soil my tongue, by speaking to a man like this.

There was a level piece of grass between us and the bog and to this place I led him. We began to wrestle and he caught me round the waist, with such a grip as never yet had been laid upon me. I heard my rib go where the pistol shot had wounded me. I wrenched at one of his arms and then I took him by the throat, which is not allowed in wrestling, but he had snatched at mine first. In two minutes I had him helpless and his blazing eyes lolled out.

"I will not harm you any more," I cried. "Carver Doone, you are beaten. Acknowledge it and thank God for it, and go your way and repent yourself."

But it was all too late. The black bog had him by the feet, and the sucking of the ground drew him on, like the thirsty lips of death. I myself just managed to leap to safety, but he fell back and, as I watched in horror, he sank gradually from sight.

Chapter XXXIX

When the little boy came back with the bluebells, which he had managed to find – as children always do find flowers, when older eyes see none – the only sign of his father left was a dark brown bubble, upon a new-formed patch of blackness.

With pain, and ache, both of mind and body, and shame at my own fury, I heavily mounted my horse again, and looked down at the innocent Ensie. Would this playful, loving child grow up like his cruel father, and end a godless life of hatred with a death of violence? He lifted his face towards me, as if to answer, "No, I will not," but the words he spoke were these: "Don" – for he never could say "John" – "oh Don, I am so glad, that nasty naughty man has gone away. Take me home, Don. Take me home." I leaned down with difficulty because of my wound, and picked him up. Then I looked around. Carver's poor horse was dead and ravens were hovering over it, the vile bog was bubbling and heaving as it consumed its prey. There was nothing to stay for and I rode slowly away.

For now I had lost a great deal of blood, and was rather faint and weary. And it was lucky for me that Kickums had lost heart, like his master, and went home as mildly as a lamb. For, when we came towards the farm, I seemed almost to be riding in a dream, and the voices of both men and women as they came rushing out, seemed to wander from a distant muffling cloud. Only the thought of Lorna's death, like a heavy knell, was tolling in the belfry of my brain.

When we came to the stable door, I rather fell from my horse than got off and John Fry, with a look of wonder, took Kickums' head and led him in while Lizzie took the child by the hand. Into the old farmhouse, I tottered like an infant, with mother helping me along.

"I have killed him," was all I said, "even as he killed Lorna. Now let me see my wife, mother. She belongs to me none the less, though dead." Annie's hand stole into mine. "John, she is not your dead one. She may even be your living one yet, your wife, your home, and your happiness. But you cannot see her yet."

"Is there any hope for her? Is there?"

"God in heaven knows, dear John. But the sight of you as you are now, would be certain death to her. Now come first and be healed yourself. Mother will care for you and I will go back to Lorna and Gwenny."

I went with mother like a child, whispering blessings on them all. Later, when I was bandaged and rested, they told me what had happened. After the shooting, Lorna was carried home at once and given into the care of Annie who refused to give up hope. She managed to extract the bullet from the wound in Lorna's side, and with the coldest

170

water cleaned it and staunched the bleeding. All this while, my darling lay unconscious and white as death, but Annie did not give up. She continued to sponge the poor side and forehead, and presently there was a little flutter in the throat, followed by a short, low sigh and Lorna opened her eyes. As soon as she did this, Annie gave her little sips of water and continued to nurse her carefully, for the danger was not yet past.

Although the doctor had set my rib, I remained weak and ill and confined to my room. I only half believed that Lorna had recovered. Seeing this, Annie tried to convince me, but I could only remember Lorna lying white and cold in the church.

"But I don't understand," I kept saying.

"You are better, dear," said Annie at last. "Will you understand if I show you Lorna? I have feared to do it for the sake of you both. But now Lorna is well enough, if you think that you are, John. Surely you will understand when you see your wife."

I felt that what she said was truth, and yet I still could not make it out. I lay in the bed and waited as in a dream and Annie left the room.

Before I had time to listen much for footsteps, Annie came back and behind her Lorna, a little shy of her bridegroom, and hanging back with her beauty. Annie banged the door and ran away and Lorna stood before me. But she did not stand for an instant when she saw what I was like; she ran into my arms although they could not hold her and she lifted my pale face up and would not look at me, having greater faith in kissing.

I felt my life come back and glow; I felt my trust in God revive; I felt the joy of living and knew that the world was good.

Little more I have to tell. The doctor came no more and

slowly my former strength came back, with a darling wife and good food. As for Lorna, she never tired of sitting watching me eat and eat. And such is her heart, that she never tires of being with me here and there, among the beautiful places, and talking, with her arm around me, of the many fears and troubles, dangers and discouragements, and worst of all the bitter partings, which we used to undergo.

Tom Faggus lost his pardon for joining the rebels at the Battle of Sedgemoor, but when a new King came, it was restored to him with the help of Jeremy Stickles who was quite happy to serve a new master. After that Tom lived a godly and righteous (though not always sober) life, cherishing dear Annie and bringing up his children to honesty above all things.

My dear mother was as happy as possibly need be with us and Lizzie married Captain Bloxham who had now succeeded to Captain Stickles' position (Jeremy having been promoted) and was happy and cheerful at last.

I sent little Ensie to Blundell's school, having changed his name for fear of what anyone might do to him. I called him Ensie Jones and hope that he will be a credit to us.

Of Lorna, of my lifelong darling, of my more and more loved wife, I will not talk, for a man should not be proud. Year by year her beauty grows, with the growth of goodness, kindness and true happiness – above all with loving, and for me it is all summed up in two words, "Lorna Doone".